Because of You, Matte Black

Freddy Gutierrez

1

ISBN 978-1-7354551-0-5

ACKNOWLEDGEMENTS

From the idea in 2011, to the first few sentences in 2015, to completion in 2020, this novel has been a crazy ride. And it wouldn't have happened without the help of everyone below, a big thank you to:

First and foremost, my beautiful wife, Holly, who has always believed in me.

My editor, Denise Baran-Unland, for the incredible work she has done in helping me bring this story to life. Her talent and creativity are unimaginable.

Tom Hernandez, for his words of wisdom and inspiration.

My brother Abel, for the amazing work he did with the cover. If you are interested in seeing what else he can do with his creative mind, hit him up at studios.elevated@gmail.com

Denise's daughter, Rebekah, for helping us put it all together.

Everyone at Write-On Joliet for opening their doors and accepting me as one of theirs.

And last but not least, my adorable dog Toki, for sitting next to me every step of the way.
Everyone's support means the world to me.

Table of Contents

Prologue

I never told anyone. They wouldn't understand.

There's nothing wrong. Everything's OK.

I lay on the floor glaring at the ceiling. My girlfriend Martia peacefully slept on her bed a few feet away. The cool desert air crept into the mobile home, raising bumps on my skin. Outside, cars came and went carelessly. Their tires crashed the asphalt like waves on a rocky beach.

There's nothing wrong. Sleep, just go to sleep.

The sparkles vanished. I danced with them throughout the night. We twirled around in the darkness for hours. We bounced against the walls, onto the ceiling, and splattered on the floor. They left me behind, tired and groggy.

I didn't want to close my eyes. I didn't want to dream. *He* lived inside me. He lurked in my head. He crawled through my thoughts and memories, turning them into living nightmares.

I didn't want to relive those days. I didn't want to feel his cold, calloused hands all over my body. But I didn't have a choice. He was always with me.

I shifted into a fetal position. I held my legs tightly, keeping myself together. Tears escaped the confinement of my eyes. They traced streams down my face and pooled on the floor by my cheeks. I stared at my girlfriend. Her bare breasts glistened under the twinkling fairy lights on the wall.

I wanted a normal life. I wanted to be normal.

There's nothing wrong, there's nothing wrong.

I closed my eyes, and everything faded to black.

I was a child again. In my nightmares, I was always a child.

I floated naked in the bathtub. I played with my rubber duckies and toy soldiers. I pushed them under and watched them float back up. I giggled and did it again. I lathered my face and head with soap bubbles. I wanted to be someone else. I wanted to be their fearless leader.

I glanced at the doorway. His eyes stared at me from the darkness of the hallway. They always glowed with lust. I looked away and pretended nothing was there. I kept playing with my toys, splashing bubbles on the tiled walls.

A shiver ran down my back and through my arms and legs until even the tips of my fingers and toes went cold.

I turned the hot water on, aching to warm up. I heard him panting in the hallway. I looked at my body beneath the water. The tub continued to fill. I picked up a duckie and rubbed his eyes.

"Don't cry duckie, there's nothing wrong," I lied.

He knelt next to me now. His hand rubbed my back and down into the water. He lined my crack with his middle finger. Shivers ran from his touch and bottlenecked at my throat.

My eyes were wet, and my face was salty. I was so cold.

I slid underwater, trying to warm up. Above me, my toys floated with the shiny bubbles. I left them behind, defenseless. Above them, his shadow hovered with desire. He waited for me to resurface. I was helpless. My eyes burned with hot, soapy pain. I shut them tight.

His hands traced up my legs.

"No! NO!" My mouth moved, but no words came out.

I opened my eyes, and I was back in Martia's room.

The morning sun snuck through the blinds on the windows. The waves picked up outside. I struggled up and wiped my face. My head pounded, and my body ached. I limped around looking for my clothes. The nightmare replayed before my eyes as I got dressed.

I grabbed my drugs and stuffed them in my backpack. Martia continued to sleep. I stood by the bed and stared at her for a moment. I thought about waking her up and telling her... I thought about begging her.

She couldn't help me. No one could.

I limped to the window and climbed out into the morning air.

Chapter 1

Why does it have to be like this? Why do the innocent always have to pay the ultimate price?

I stood by the shoulder and stared at a dying skunk on the road. It scratched at the asphalt, gnawing its tongue in pain. Blood flowed away from its body and crusted on the gravel. What a merciless death for such a marvelous creature. I saw it just minutes ago looking for food in the arroyo. I kept my distance, watching curiously. I followed it out to the streets. It sniffed by the shoulder for a few minutes, hesitating as it crossed the road.

Now, I'm witnessing its last few breaths.

The idiot who hit it played on their phone instead of paying attention to what was ahead. It happens too often on these lone country roads. There's no authority to enforce the law that protects the innocent, not from stupid anyway.

I looked up at the car that hit it, a grandma gold sedan with a "My child is an honor roll student at Abbott High School" bumper sticker. It sped away, still swerving left and right. *So selfish*. That person could have hit anything or anyone today, but it hit that poor animal instead.

That could've been me.

I wish it would've been me.

The skunk twitched and screamed, spewing a mixture of blood and urine, still trying to defend itself. It never stood a chance. Modern machinery always wins against mother nature.

I gazed at it a little longer thinking about its life. How old was it? Did it have babies? Will they die, too, now that they can't feed on their own? It's sad, but it is the inevitability of life I suppose.

Hmm, life… what a fucking joke.

I try to do what's right. I try to be a good guy. I've tried again and again to ignore the fact life is nothing but pain. I've tried to pretend as if the world around me isn't collapsing little by little. But every day, things like these make me face reality, and force me to accept that it is.

Life's not fair.

I knelt by the animal, a little too close to the road, so no one could hit it again. Or maybe hit us both, I don't know. But there were no other cars in sight. I sat with my legs crossed before me, just waiting. After a little while, its breathing slowed down. Its mouth dried out and its feet stopped moving. Its eyes were wet and glossy.

Can animals cry?

I got back on my feet and took a deep breath. I picked the animal up by the tail. Its body was still soft and warm. I scurried to some bushes a few feet from the road and gently lay the body. I felt like I should say something, anything.

"I'm sorry." My voice was coarse and strange.

I turned back to the road and continued my walk to work.

I kicked rocks that crossed my path, trying to forget what I just witnessed. If only I could be a robot like one of my cybernetic idols, I could erase the footage from my memory. I'd erase the images of the car hitting the skunk. I'd erase the painful screeches it made as it lay dying.

I'd erase my nightmares.

Growing up, I'd watch a lot of TV. I'd watch cartoons and movies about lifeless humanoids. Saturday mornings, I'd plop my ass in front of the TV with a bowl of off-brand cereal. I'd use whatever clean bowl or bowl-like container I could find. I remember watching as much television as I could before my father woke up and our living room turned into an active war zone.

Those robots, though. They had it right. Their sleek metal bodies and inability to feel pain were always my favorite attributes. I marveled at their strength and callous behavior. I fantasized about being like them for many years. I built armors out of cardboard and sticks, taped up with stickers and magic tape. I'd suit up every day in the blistering heat and fight my demons with homemade weaponry until I accepted that they couldn't be defeated. My cybernetic idols were part of a make-believe world.

They couldn't save me any more than I could save myself. I had to grow up.

I saw the West Public Library up ahead. The sandy wilderness came to a stop before the packed parking lot. Oh, that parking lot, it had definitely seen better days. Now it probably had more holes than the surface of the moon. On hot sunny days, I liked to imagine I was walking in a post-battle field. Each hole was created by a landmine who exploded trying to keep people out.

When it rained, the holes collected water that turned them into mirrors. I loved looking at the sky reflected at them. I daydreamed about jumping in and instantly being transported to a different dimension where I could be a normal guy, with a normal life.

The library was a red brick building that was as old and tired as the town I called home. It reminded me of grade school: shitty food and shifty people. I even got that same sunken feeling in my gut every time I saw it. I cringed at the thought of going through those dirty glass doors.

Don't get me wrong. My job was simple, catalogue the books that were dropped off and issue out new ones to those who were interested in expanding their minds. The hours were odd, and the staff was crazy, but at least I had weekends off.

The job itself wasn't strict. It wasn't a pain the ass to go to work on Monday mornings. On most days, it didn't even require me to interact with the patrons. All I had to do was show up, follow the steps that were ingrained in my brain from day one, and look alive.

Look alive… that was the hardest thing to do. How could I look alive if I didn't even want to be alive? But I couldn't kill myself either. I didn't have the balls to do it. As my cybernetic organism idol would say, I could not self-terminate.

I was a failure who never accomplished anything. I was a loser who quit college and lived at his parent's house. I was in and out of fucked up relationships, and to top it off, I didn't even have friends to talk about it. Here I was, this twenty-one year – old college dropout who couldn't get shit right if his life depended on it. I was wasted space.

I walked in with my eyes glued to the floor. My shoelaces fluttered around trying to escape my feet. If I didn't make eye contact with anyone, I wouldn't have to say a word the entire day. Perfect.

I snuck by the front counter into the employee breakroom. I dropped off my stuff in my locker and grabbed my name tag. I glanced at the schedule posted on the fridge door. It was my day to arrange the Children's section This would be an easy day.

"Nice shirt," Malinda said.

I looked down at my shirt. I was literally wearing the same shirt yesterday. In fact, I had been wearing the same black shirt, hoodie, and washed out blue jeans all week. What did she mean *nice* shirt?

"Umm thanks. Nice dress."

Malinda wore a navy churchy dress with a grey sweater. She was definitely dressed for the job she had.

"Thanks," she replied, pointing her nose up.

She pushed past me to get to the schedule.

"Yay! Front desk!" She clapped her hands and skipped out the breakroom.

Malinda had started at the West Public Library about a year after me. From our first encounter, I could tell it would be hard to get along with her. That morning we reached for the front door at the same time. "Ew," was her literal response as I opened the door for her. Can you imagine that? Someone being so grossed out by you that they felt the need to say, "Ew?" I couldn't either till it happened to me.

Her demeanor changed once she saw we'd be coworkers.

With time she remembered me. We had attended West High together, graduated the same year. But we were part of two different worlds. She was the pretty, popular girl while I was the misfit. Her life had completely changed after the unwanted pregnancy senior year. It basically ruined her life. Now, she was barely a step above me.

Oh, sweet, naïve, Malinda. Never change, girl.

I pinned my name tag on my shirt, put my earphones in, and followed her out.

Every day I saw them; the hipsters, starving artists, millennials, whatever you wanna call them. Day by day they came into the library with their vintage leather bookbags and expensive coffee drinks. They sat in the most populated areas of the library and "read" their 500-plus page novels written by some local, obscure author. I knew they weren't really reading. It's impossible to read when you sit in the pathways that everybody uses to get around. Shit, sometimes it's impossible to read in the comfort of your own home. I knew they just wanted some chump to see them and envy them, secretly wishing he was like them.

Yes, I was that chump. I always wanted what they had. I wanted it so bad, I purposely tried to be the complete opposite of them. I grew out my hair until it was a shaggy mess and wore the same clothes year after year. My hoodie was faded, and my jeans had more holes than the cool designer jeans in the mall had.

I tried so hard to change who I was just so people wouldn't compare me to them. But what was the point? I was the only one who compared myself to them. I spent years mentally torturing myself, scrutinizing every aspect of my existence, trying to figure out who I was, who I wanted to be, and who I would never be. It was time lost and, as we all know, time is unforgiving.

I had been working at West Public Library for a couple of years. Earning that job was literally the only lucky strike I ever had. My mother always wanted me to succeed in life. She hated that I had quit college and was working in construction with my father. I knew it wasn't the life she wanted for me.

I remember the day like it was yesterday. My mother drove us to the library to meet her childhood friend, the library director. My mother was convinced her friend could get me a job. As she yapped about it, I looked out the window and stared at the road. The asphalt carved away at the car tires as the miles rolled away. I wondered what it would do to my skin if I was to jump out.

"This is a good opportunity, Aiden. This is a good job. If you get in, you won't have to be out in the sun all day."

"I don't mind the sun."

"That's not what I mean. You just seem so tired when you get home. Working outside... it's just not for you."

"I used to garden with Grandma all the time. I like it."

"Damn it, Aiden. It's not the same." She gripped the steering wheel hard enough to drain her hands of blood.

She shot her eyes at me. They were crisp bluish-grey, tired like my Grandma's.

"Listen, hon, just give it a try. If you don't like it, then you can go back to working with your dad."

I knew exactly what she meant. She didn't want to see her firstborn son miserable, tired, and filthy to the point of being unrecognizable every day. But most importantly, she didn't want her son to follow his father's footsteps and become a raging alcoholic. But that was out of her control. Like father, like son.

That day, I saw my mother inside Mrs. Robinson's office. She was smaller when standing next to a woman of power. She waved her arms and smiled a shy, fake smile. It was more of a polite gesture rather than a smile. They looked at me and looked at each other several times. I knew this was a big favor to ask.

I walked around the lobby, trying to envision myself working there. I couldn't. Stressed out mothers with their children tugging at their pants took up the main areas. Their screechy voices made my skin crawl. The computer room was crowded, and teenagers were sitting on the walkways. So. Many. People. I couldn't be around that many people. They made my stomach hurt.

I stopped by the news board and noticed a poster about a writing contest brought to West by the local newspaper in partnership with the University of Texas at Arlington. The contest had been over for a month. Beneath the original post, the winners name was typed in silver glitter in an added post. First prize winner: Tommy Robinson.

Turns out, Tommy was Mrs. Robinson's son.

The prize was to travel the world to see the most romantic places it had to offer; Italy, Spain, France, Rome, Japan, Cancun, and Cleveland amongst others. A total of twenty-two locations were to be seen in sixty days.

On the counter under the news board sat a pile of pamphlets with all the entries. I picked one up and browsed through it. I was curious to see what Tommy had written. I flipped through the pages until I found his entry.

Tommy wrote about falling in love. He wrote about meeting his girlfriend and how his breath escaped his body every time he saw her. He said his body filled with thousands of tiny bubbles that lifted him and carried him to a place where nothing mattered. He explained how everything fell into place when he was with her. The title: The power of love.

I thought about the days when we attended school together. He was always a joyous boy. I saw his words in my memories of him. When he was with her, he had the world at his fingertips. He walked differently. He spoke differently. They walked around smiling and giggling, hanging onto each other. They stared into each other's eyes and kissed gently. He lifted her up and carried her in his arms effortlessly. His perfect life made me sad.

Feeling that way about anyone was unimaginable to me.

After Tommy won the contest, his girlfriend quit her job at the library to accompany him on his trip. In her fairytale head, she hoped they would get lucky and be offered to stay in *le Paris*. In my sad reality, Mrs. Robinson gave me her job. Like I said, I was in luck that day.

That was so long ago. Time really flies when you're having *fun*.

My workday was a breeze. Music and books melted away the hours. Before I knew it, it was time to leave.

Every night at 7 p.m. Martia would swing by and pick me up out back by the dumpster. I never got my license, never had any interest to do so. I always thought of it as another way of control. When driving a motor vehicle, you surrender all control and basically allow chance to take your life. Thousands of people are on the streets at any given time, every single one of them gambling their lives away. If I couldn't take my own life, why should I allow someone else to?

I snuck out nightly through the back door to avoid contact with my fellow employees. I just couldn't bear the idea of having meaningless conversations with them. It was pointless. I didn't like them, and they didn't like me, so why pretend like we had an interest in each other's lives? It was another one of those stupid little things adults did that never made any sense.

I leaned against the dumpster and scrolled through my phone. The dumpster at the library was by far the cleanest dumpster any establishment could have. It smelled like paper with

14

a hint of rotting banana. Trash always smells like banana even if there are no bananas in it. Have you ever noticed that?

Martia rolled up in her beater '96 coupe, music blaring and muffler farting. The mobile beat box had been her father's before hers. He had given it to her after he purchased a newer version of the same car, same color and all. They both gave the poor thing hell. I was surprised it was still running.

I hopped in the passenger seat. The car smelled like cigarettes and cheap dollar store body spray, *Enchanted Forest*. She tried so hard to hide the stench. It was easier to stop smoking, probably cheaper too. But logic wasn't Martia's forte. I put my seatbelt on, and Martia smacked her lips at me. She turned up the music and stepped on the gas.

Every night Martia fed me a tuna fish sandwich on the way to her place. She thought she was being thoughtful. I hated tuna fish. I never even liked sea food but as much as I explained that to her, she never listened. I always ate it anyway. It was easier just to eat it than to never hear the end of why I refused to eat her food.

Martia's parents worked the second shift at a plastic molding company and were generally gone from 5 p.m. to 2 a.m. Like many others in the small town of West, Texas, they were losers without aspirations who cemented themselves in the same job their whole lives.

They worked their shitty job during the week and partied like there was no tomorrow on the weekends. Because there wasn't; in their meaningless lives, Tomorrow never came. It was the same bullshit every week of every year. The same bullshit life their offspring would grow up to follow.

I spent most of my time at Martia's house. It was an escape from the personal hell at my house. I was tired of the lack of affection and my parent's constant physical altercations. I was tired of walking on eggshells every day, simply to avoid making things worse. It's impossible to get used to a loveless life.

At Martia's, every night was the same. The second we walked through the door, she'd want to rip my clothes off. It was like clockwork. It didn't matter if I was in the mood or not.

"Oh, what a day. Here, catch." Martia said, tossing me a beer.

I dropped my backpack on the floor and leaned against the wall, sliding down to the cheap linoleum. I opened my beer and took a sip. *Ahhh, pisswater.* She sat on her bed and popped one open herself. She rested the sweaty can on her nightstand and opened the top drawer. She took some molly and washed it down with another sip of beer. I stared at her, watching the drugs take effect.

Martia wore daisy dukes with flip flops and a white tank top. She lay on the bed and began rubbing her legs from her ankles to her inner thighs. She threw her head back and rubbed her breasts, making her nipples hard. She looked towards me and bit her bottom lip.

"C'mon, baby, let's get you out of those. Mamma wants some dick."

I got up and slowly walked up to her. I chugged my beer and threw the can on the floor.

"C'mon, take it off. I want you now."

I smiled a crooked smile, the alcohol already taking effect.

"Your sister is literally ten feet out that door."

"Psst, like I care. Fat bitch prolly gets off hearing us."

Martia put a molly in my mouth. I swallowed it dry. She laughed and licked my stomach. She yanked my jeans and boxers off hard, and then dug her nails into my ass cheeks while pushing my dick in her mouth. I knew her nails drew blood. I felt a little dribble running down my leg.

I never told her how much her *love* hurt. They were more than just wounds to the flesh. They were constant reminders of the life that I lived. They were the vile things that lead me to her, and kept me at her side.

I fucked her every night. I fucked her hard and raw in every single square inch of her room. We fucked and did drugs. We danced around in the silent darkness until one of us passed out. Most of the time, she gave in first, and I would be left alone to battle my thoughts. They were battles I never won, battles that made me sick, battles I hated fighting again and again.

Every night was the same.

I saw Martia sleeping naked next to me in bed. I stared down at my naked body. I looked around at her room and the life we had created. This was it. This was the peak of our existence. Sex and drugs in a shitty trailer home.

I climbed out of bed and onto the floor. I crawled on my hands and knees to the darkest, emptiest part of her room. I took a couple of LSD-soaked paper strips from my backpack and placed them on my tongue. I closed my eyes and clenched my jaw, waiting for my body to dissolve.

When I reopened them, I was instantly surrounded by sparkles of a billion colors. I stared at the walls as they engulfed me and took me to a place that existed only in those LSD strips. Each sparkle was its own galaxy, each harboring a planet where a different version of me lived a better life than me. I floated with them, clashing and splashing without a care in *my* world.

In Martia's hell, it was always the same. Every hellish relationship I had was always the same. The girls were always party monsters with no self-esteem. I was always the same worthless soul, the sex fiend who had nothing to offer besides his dick.

The night would end, and my day would begin, only to be the same all over again.

Chapter 2

Nothing super exciting ever happened at the library. I spent most of my days alone in the aisles with mountains of books, lost in lyrics and music. I loved music. I loved how artists could pour their hearts into songs and create the perfect story in just three and a half minutes. I loved how the same song meant something different for everyone that heard it.

Mrs. Robinson and Malinda rarely ever bothered me. I communicated with them mostly with shrugs and nods. Patrons mostly avoided me. They only spoke to me when they had to on the days I worked the checkout counter.

Then there were those *other* days. The ones filled with longing to be a hipster while cleaning the man juice off the keyboards in the computer room. Yes, man juice. Those sick freaks had no shame, but I somehow didn't mind.

I saw each one come into the library several times a week. They walked up and down the aisles until the computer room was nearly empty and then they moved in. I ran virus scans on some computers as they chose empty ones in the farthest section from the entrance. I pretended to wipe the counters as they'd cover themselves with whatever they had. Some used their sweaters, others magazines, and others their backpacks. They typed the website address and went to town.

It was as if they had this unspoken agreement. They all knew what each other was doing. But they never made any sort of contact with one another. They just did it, in the same room, in the middle of the day.

The internet service in West was the worst. It was expensive and unreliable. Being an educational institute, the library had the best internet service in town. That was as good as it got. We charged $5 per hour to use the internet in the computer room. So to watch porn and bust a nut every other day seemed like a fair price. With dick in hand, not even becoming an exhibitionist mattered.

I walked around checking off cleaning and software installation logs, purposely waiting for them to do their deed and leave. But they were silent jackers. Sometimes I didn't even hear them leave. I'd look up to catch a glimpse of dick or flying jizz and they'd be already gone.

After they left, I looked for the keyboards that were soaked in the semen of the unknown men. I ran my bare fingers across the keys, feeling the cold gelatinous material against my skin. I raised my fingers up to my face, and I smelled it. I let it fill my lungs as I imagined the men in their public moment of bliss. I didn't know why I did it, and I couldn't understand why I liked it.

It was just one of those things.

That day, oh that glorious day, I'll never forget *that day*. I was arranging books against the preteen wall, minding my own business. I had my earphones in, blasting one of my favorite songs. My eyes were closed, and I was so into the song that I didn't even notice I had started swaying. I banged my head side to side while moving my hips left and right. I threw my hands up in the air and allowed the music to flow through me.

The song ended and the next started, bringing me back to reality. I realized how careless I had been. I opened my eyes and looked around hoping no one had seen my actions. But someone had. One person had seen me in the most embarrassing moment of my life.

Four shelves down, a young man stared at me from the mystery section. He offered a shy, modest smile. Fuck.

He stood tall and slim; his hair was cut short on the sides and back. The top was long, black and swept across his face. His eyes hid behind his dark-rimmed glasses. He wore a Vinyl's band T-shirt and tight grey jeans.

Fuck! Shit! I'm an idiot! FUUUCKK!

19

I casually strolled to the magazine rack and flipped through the magazines, playing it cool. I'd look up every few seconds, for just a half second to see if he still looked in my direction. He did. He took out books and put them back on the shelves, glancing up between them. I realized he wouldn't let that one die. At least he wasn't recording me as I danced around like a fucking idiot. I glanced back up and noticed him walking towards me.

Fuck! He's walking this way. He's probably going to laugh in my face. I have to take my break. I have to take my break. Go take your break, what are you doing?!

I threw the magazine I was holding onto the rack and hurried towards the breakroom.

I sensed his eyes following me as I nearly sprinted across the library. He would definitely not let that one go. I shook the thoughts away and fast-walked by Malinda and Mrs. Robinson at the front desk. They both stared at me wondering what the fuck I was doing.

The employee breakroom at the library was much nicer than my own home. The room had a giant 55-inch TV mounted on the wall, a full living room set, and a kitchenette ready to prepare full meals.

On the wall by the door, there were glossy blue lockers where we kept personal items. We were told to decorate our own to show our spirit. Stickers of kittens and puppies, stars and inspirational quotes littered Malinda's. A few others had some stickers but nothing compared to Malinda's. Mine only had a sticker with my name written in Mrs. Robinson's perfect handwriting.

I threw myself on the couch and closed my eyes. I felt safe. Patrons weren't allowed in the breakroom. Not once in my tenure at the library had someone walked in there. I thought about taking a short snooze to help me forget my embarrassing moment. But I couldn't sleep. The constant stream of self-destructive thoughts made it impossible to drift off. And the sparkles wouldn't come unless I called for them. But that was out of the question. I had made it a rule not to do drugs in public.

Oh, how I loved torturing myself.

So I got up, and to my surprise, caught the exact moment when my life changed forever. Walking in the door was none other than the mysterious young man. I was starstruck. I couldn't move, and I couldn't breathe. He gracefully sauntered across the room and sat on the loveseat across from me. He was so cool and he knew it.

"Hey," he said. His voice was soft and mellow, like Jesus Christ's might sound.

He lay his phone and water bottle on the coffee table and stared at me. My heart was beating so fast, I couldn't process the situation.

Seriously? The breakroom? Why couldn't he walk into the computer room instead?!

"You... you can't be back here."

The thought of having him in front of me stopped all other thoughts from going forward.

"Relax, it's cool," he said.

"No, get the fuck out of here. This room is for employees only."

"Dude, I've worked here for like a month already."

Impossible! I shook my head and stared at the floor. I scanned the days in my head to see if by any chance I had seen him.

"You're lying! I've never seen you here. Now get out before I call the cops," I said, pointing towards the door.

"What's going on in here, boys?"

Mrs. Robinson came into the room, holding her glasses in one hand and her phone in the other. Her curly hair was pulled into a ponytail, and she wore a tight, flowery dress.

"Aiden... Matthew? Either of you care to explain?"

"My name is Matte." He adjusted his glasses under his fringe, still glaring at me.

"I don't believe in nicknames, young man. I call people by their given name."

"I understand, but my name is not Matthew. My name is Matte... M-a-t-t-e."

Mrs. Robinson was speechless. She raised an eyebrow and shook her head trying to comprehend.

"Well, *Matte*, what is the problem here? I heard shouting." Mrs. Robinson put her glasses on and continued to stare us down.

"Mrs. Robinson, tell him he's not allowed in the employee breakroom," I interrupted.

She looked at me with a "what the fuck is wrong with you" face.

"Aiden, honey, *Matte* here is an employee. He's been working here for a little over a month now. Have you two not met?"

"No, I've never seen him before!"

"Sweetie, calm down. He's going to be filling in for Mrs. Cooper while she's out on medical leave."

Six weeks ago, Mrs. Cooper had tripped over a hipster and fell to the floor, breaking a knee. I had been completely oblivious to a replacement. At the time all I could think was, how can anyone get hurt at the library?

Matte collected his phone and water bottle, smirking at me. He stood and strolled to the door, apologizing to Mrs. Robinson for the disturbance.

"Now, are you going to behave, or do you need to go home?"

"I'm sorry. I seriously thought he was an intruder. It won't happen again."

"Good." She grinned and patted my back.

I didn't see Matte for the rest of the afternoon. I wondered if he had he left for the day, or if he was purposely avoiding me. I don't blame him. I must have seemed like a total nutcase. I mean seriously, who makes a scene like that?

Whatever it was, his impact cleared my head enough to notice the changes at the library.

Out on the floor, I noticed new chairs and tables. The blinds on the windows were gone, revealing the desert landscape outside. Glittery Easter egg cutouts on the shelves and baskets with bright colored eggs by the main counter were obvious decoration choices by Malinda. New posters plastered the walls, and Mrs. Robinson had lost some weight.

I couldn't remember the last time I had been out of my head.

Although I didn't see him again, he lingered in my mind. He was so different than everyone I had encountered at the library.

He was so cool. I liked his style. I wasn't a fan of the Vinyl's, but to each his own.

I looked up some songs on my phone and listened to them as I continued to work. The more I listened, the more they grew on me. I guess they weren't *that* bad. Each song helped time melt away. Each song brought new questions. Why hadn't I noticed him before? What other music did he like? Had he noticed *me* before? Had he seen me, dancing around like an idiot before? *God, I hope not.*

So many questions... about him bounced around in my head. Him. Why was he in my head? It was 7 p.m. before I knew it. I gathered my belongings and snuck out the back.

Martia was parked by the dumpster. She sat in her car, smoking a cigarette. She smiled and flicked the butt at me as I walked up.

Chapter 3

For over a decade, I walked through life in a nightmare from which I couldn't wake up. Every day was a struggle. The ghosts that accumulated in my head broke me down. The very substances that silenced them were also silently killing... *me*. It was a vicious battle I could not win.

The next day I walked into the library with a fresh set of eyes. Malinda was decorating the entry way with pictures of beach balls and palm trees. She wore a short, flowy lilac dress and a large white hat with a hibiscus flower on it. Mrs. Robinson had on bright pink sunglasses and a navy polo with khaki shorts.

"Aiden, what the heck?" Malinda looked pissed.

"What?"

"You're wearing *that* again. It's beach day. Didn't you get the memo I sent out?"

I looked down at my hoodie, black T-shirt, and washed-out blue jeans. Fourth day in a row.

"Sorry, guess I didn't."

Malinda threw her hands in the air and shook her head shamefully.

I grabbed my name tag from my locker in the employee breakroom. It was Thursday morning; my day to collect the books in the outside drop basket. I grabbed the empty cart and wheeled it outside.

Although it was the first week of May, the temperature was already a sweltering 90 degrees. By the end of May, it would be well over 100 degrees. Regardless of the season in West, Texas, it was winter every day. Everything in this sepia town remained as dead as always.

As I unlocked the drop box and wheeled out the cart full of books, the familiar sound of approaching hipsters surrounded me. They walked past me, reeking of coffee and witch-hazel, the unmistakable scent of new-age beauty. They were the kings and queens of western suburbia.

Like an army of clones, they marched to the library, never missing a step. Oh, how I wanted to be them! I would give my left nut for at least a day in their struggle-free lives.

"This coffee is disgusting," one guy said. He rocked a buzz-cut and his beard nearly connected with his oversized sunglasses. His plaid shirt looked like a 1950's tablecloth, and his pants were tight enough for me to see the mushroom print. "Let me guess, you didn't use deionized water heated to exactly 132 degrees, did you?"

"We should've seriously just gone to Starbies, this is horrendous!" exclaimed another tartan king. His beard wasn't as bushy, and his pompadour reflected the morning sun like a silver streak.

"Oh. My. God. What the fuck is that?" asked a girl pushing up her glassless glasses.

My embarrassing trance broke as I noticed what the hipster girl was gasping at. Out of my cart, a cloud of tiny pieces fluttered away with the wind. I chopstick-ed one of the pieces with my fingers in mid-air and found a veiny dick printed on it. I scrunched my eyebrows.

Within a matter of seconds all the flying pieces revealed the naked human flesh printed on them. Somebody had shredded an erotic magazine and dumped it into the cart.

Mortified, I grabbed the cart handle and ran past the hipsters. Books flew out with every bump the cart hit on the sidewalk. Behind me, a wave of laughter erupted. I left the cart by the entrance and ran to the men's room. I hid in a stall, hoping to die.

I listened carefully for any signs of laughter. I could barely hear them, but they were there. I covered my ears with my hands, trying to make them disappear.

After nearly thirty minutes, the restroom door opened. Footsteps squeaked past the urinals and stopped by the stalls. Silence followed. A few seconds later, comfort arrived.

"Dude, it's gonna be alright. I took care of it," the soft, mellow voice of Jesus Christ said.

I remained silent while the footsteps made their way to the door. As it crept open, he spoke again. "You can come out whenever you're ready."

The door closed, and silence remained.

I sat on the toilet and stared at my shoes. This was a mess. This was a shitty fucking way to start another shitty fucking day. There was no way in hell people would let this one die. Not in this boring town. No way.

My eyes wandered off and got caught by something on the wall. Somebody had actually painted graffiti at the library. How uninspiring. I got closer to read what it said. The small red print said: Matte likes dick.

Matte likes dick?

The thought intrigued me and I wondered if it was true. Who could've wrote that? Maybe a friend? Or maybe an ex? I rubbed the words with my hand and shook my head.

I eventually left the restroom and returned to work. The hipsters never stayed past noon, which meant no more hiding. When I got out to the floor, Malinda and Mrs. Robinson had turned the entire library into a beach resort. They had placed cardboard palm trees across the library and even put up a tiki hut by the children's play area.

I wasn't in the mood for nonsense. I reported to my station and ignored everything else. Everything was better for me when I followed the routines.

As I stocked my way through the young adult section, something inside me yearned to encounter Jesus Christ again. I wanted his soothing voice to calm me down and bring me back to Earth. But as the hours passed, the mysterious young man failed to make another appearance.

Instead, he lingered in my mind. Could he be... *gay*? Nah, he didn't look like it. I mean, the guy had serious punk vibes. I wondered what he was wearing today. Maybe another band T-shirt? I thought about other bands he might like. The music app in my phone recommended similar music. I put them on auto play and listened my day away to classic rock bands.

At around 6:50 p.m. I texted Martia.

"I won't need a ride tonight. I'll be going home. I need rest."

She immediately texted back, "K". She was probably getting ready to leave. Good thing I caught her before she did. Had she been outside, she'd probably be pissed. I didn't have time for meaningless arguments. I needed to think.

At 7 p.m. I gathered my belongings and snuck out the back door. This was the first time in two years that I did something different. Change made me uneasy. That's why I always avoided it. But something inside told me it was time for something new. It was inevitable, change was already in motion.

The sun had started its descent into the horizon. I had about an hour of light. It would be enough to make it to my house without having to worry about wild animals.

I jumped into the arroyo that led to the reservoir. The reservoir was the most secluded area of town. It was decorated with more trees and shrubs than any park around. It was an oasis in the middle of a wasteland.

Being a desert town, West had crazy flashfloods during the storm season. Drainage ditches carried the water to the reservoir after the storms. The rest of the days, the arroyos were like massive, dried-up riverbeds. The ripples on the sandy bottom marked the crazy waters. Every storm carved its own depth in each ditch.

The deep trenches that expanded to and from the reservoir were like giant mazes where anyone could explore. They welcomed punks to drink and do drugs. They instigated middle schoolers to break bottles and shoot wildlife with BB guns. They invited high school kids to explore their sexuality. The reservoir was on the way to my house.

I kicked dirt and beer bottles as I trudged. There was always something out of the ordinary in the arroyos. When it wasn't a decaying animal corpse, it was a piece of technology that was as old as I was. Of course, other unusual stuff like needles and latex contraceptives could always be found.

Before long, sure enough, the first condom wrapper crossed my path. I stepped on it; seminal fluids squirted out. It was old and watery. I fought the urge to stick around and kept plodding.

In the distance, I saw a pickup truck partly hidden behind tall bushes. Next to the parked truck, a young man and woman hurriedly got dressed. I continued walking towards them, imagining what they were doing. I slowed my pace, giving them time to leave. My stomach twisted in nervous knots. By the time I reached the spot, they'd already sped off.

Two condom wrappers lay between the tire tracks. These were fresh. I picked one up and pulled the condom right out. It was bloody and warm, the remains of someone's innocence. Thoughts of the young couple wrapped in each other's arms flashed before my eyes. I imagined them undressing one another nervously. They stumbled a few times as they tried hard to not make fools out of themselves on their first encounter. Their breath was heavy, their minds were focused on the final goal. They explored each other. It was all new to them. They kissed and licked, tasting the other's sweetness. He rolled the condom on his dick, and they began their journey to ecstasy.

I carefully untied the condom keeping the contents inside. I saw my hands moving as if they had a mind of their own. I placed two fingers inside and allowed the ejaculate to saturate them. I could almost feel the young man trembling with pleasure as he came.

What am I doing?

I dropped the condom. I wiped my fingers on my pants and stumbled away. My eyes dropped, and my throat knotted.

I spun around and lunged for the second wrapper, shaking uncontrollably. My hands unzipped my pants and pulled out my dick. One hand stroked while the other brought the condom to my mouth. My teeth undid the knot, tears welled up. I placed the used condom on my erection and proceeded to masturbate. The ejaculate of the previous user swished back and forth, coating my member in undeniable sin. I stroked harder and faster. My breath escaped my body. My tears raced down my cheeks, falling to the sand, and just as I ejaculated, I collapsed behind them.

I hated myself. I wanted to tear my skin off and become someone else, anyone else. I tossed the condom aside and got up. I pulled my pants up and turned to run away. Wiping my face, not once did I look back.

When will it be over? When will I no longer walk the world with the weight of my past on my shoulders?

The second I got home, I ran straight to the bathroom and stripped naked. I wanted the sparkles to come and hold me. I wanted to live in a world where everything would be all right, where something as idealistic as hope still existed.

I placed two strips in my mouth and locked the door. My mother called out to me, but her words dissolved through my head. My brother banged on the door as the knocks echoed in my chest. I turned the water on as hot as I could and jumped in.

The drops danced around my body, and the steam tried to comfort me.

"Clean me!" I begged them.

Every nerve ending in my body was alive with pleasure, with pain. My thoughts melted, and my tears drowned within the scorching shower. My life scattered around me waiting to be put back together. I tried to scream but swallowed my words instead. No one could hear my cries. No one would feel my pain.

No one could know what he did to me.

Outside the door, I heard commotion. Angry screams of a prideful father. Begging cries of a fearful mother. His blows to her flesh were jagged melodies to my ears. My brother slammed on the door, desperate for my attention. The poor thing was only seven. Each year of his life was progressively worse. His youth was wasted in that broken home.

I got dressed in the same dirty clothes and opened the door. My brother hugged me. His tears soaked through my shirt. He grabbed my hand, pulled me to the hallway, and hid behind me. I saw them like silhouettes in broken light. He beat her, and she took it. He beat her, and I lost it. I lunged at him, my body in slow motion. I knocked him to the floor and jumped onto him. Over and over, I punched his face without feeling a thing. His blood spattered in beautiful splashes of color.

His face was dough beneath my fists. I continued until there was no struggle. I continued until I could no more. My brother held my mother. They stared at the animal I had become.

Their faces were stretched beyond recognition. They shivered with uncertainty, silently questioning if I would attack them, too.

The walls wobbled with uneven patterns. But to be fair, they had never offered a sturdy home. I stood and waddled away, my footsteps following me closely until the bloody ink ran out.

Chapter 4

Nature gave me a comfortable place to sleep off the events of last night. The grass kept me cushioned, and the morning dew cleansed my face. I sat up and felt the full weight of the night. My jaw ached. I was probably clenching it in my sleep. I do that sometimes.

Nothing would wipe away my actions. Nothing would allow me to forget. The bruises and scratches, the evidence, were written on me.

I tried to familiarize myself with my surroundings. Some trees in the distance, a couple swing sets, a sandbox, a big slide, and a small slide. I was at the West Texas Memorial Site. The sad excuse for a park housed my happiest memories.

During my early childhood, my mother took me to the park a lot. I remember playing with her trying to catch bubbles. I remember her pushing me on the swing. I'd scream, "Higher! Higher!"

She waited for me when I slid down the tall metal slide. I don't know why I wanted to go down that slide. I could've gone down the little kid one. But no, I insisted on this one. And she let me. I guess I just wanted to show her I could. So, I went up the tall ladder. I stood at the very top and waved. She waved back. I was up so high, and I was so scared. But I did it. I closed my eyes and went down. The air blew my hair and the metal burned my legs.

I remember crying when I reached the bottom. My mother picked me up and carried me to the sandbox. She tried to console me, but I cried louder. This was a different type of pain. I didn't cry because my legs burned. I cried because I felt unhinged, like suddenly everything pressed down on me.

And then I stopped. Just like that. I got up and ran into the field like nothing had happened. I started stomping on dandelions and chasing squirrels. My mother stood a few feet away, staring at me. We were so young back then. There was still so much more we had to live through. There was still so much more we had to suffer.

I loved the park. It was no wonder in my stupor I ended up there.

But today my knees didn't have grass stains, and I wasn't winded by activity. I wore the stains of my father's blood on my arms like the birthmarks life had given me. They were dark and crusty.

I have to get out of here.

Being bloody and disoriented in the park wasn't a good idea if I wanted to avoid jail. So, I did what my gut told me not to do and struggled to my feet. I had to go to Martia's house. Inwardly, I cringed. It was too early for that shit. Just being around her was nauseating. But as much as I hated it, she was always the way out. She was my one way to forget, even if she wasn't.

One year later, I still didn't know how I ended up with her. The clouds lurking over my head always prevented me from seeing the real her. All I ever saw were the drugs that always made it all go away. She was the one drug I couldn't quit.

My mind was so clogged with thoughts and memories, I could scarcely breathe. I wanted them out, I wanted to forget everything.

I limped out of the grass and across the street. I walked the back alleys, fighting each step. On an average day, I was as low as the ground beneath my feet. With Martia, I was six feet under. She was going straight to hell, but I would see her there, because we… we were the same.

Birds chirped happily and squirrels ran around chasing each other. Residents watered their trees and gardens in their backyards. They watched me and judged me as I limped past them. They peered through my flesh, muscles, and bones, straight into my broken soul. They were everywhere; at the library, at the store, in the streets, in the alleys, in my head… I could not escape them.

It was Judgment Day. Every. Day.

About twenty minutes later, I stumbled into Martia's backyard. The mobile home creaked as occupants stomped around inside. Martia screamed obscenities at her sister, just a typical day. Her voice echoed in my head, pounding my brain.

I sat on the patchy grass and leaned against a tree. I needed a moment of silence and peace. The sun beat down on me hard. Sweat poured out of my head and ran down my face and neck. I stared down at my sore hands. They trembled with pain and discomfort.

Not five minutes later, Martia came outside, holding two garbage bags. She looked straight at me and continued to the trash cans in the alley. She dumped the bags and walked back to the door. Her flip flops slapped my ears. When she climbed up the steps, she paused and turned again.

"Are you coming in, or you gonna stay out here all day?" she asked.

I sighed.

I struggled to my feet and limped inside.

Her family sat at the kitchen table, getting ready to eat breakfast. The smell of coffee and grease tickled my nose. The TV in the next room played the morning news loudly. There was a moment of quiet gasps as I walked through the door, an obvious reaction to the blood stains all over my body.

Fuck my life.

I avoided eye contact and looked at my feet as we walked past them. My shoes were bloody and muddy. My shoelaces dragged behind me. I guess they wanted breakfast. I was kinda hungry too.

I sensed her family's eyes following me until I disappeared into Martia's bedroom. That was nothing out of the ordinary. Her parents and older sister always looked down on me for my questionable choices in life. They either wondered why in the hell I was with Martia, or why in God's name she was with me.

We never spent any time together, getting to know each other. All they knew about me was what they saw and what Martia told them. All I knew about them was just what I pieced together; when they were home, when they were gone, and the ID badges they left hanging by the front door. Martia never spoke about them.

I closed the bedroom door behind me. The familiar stank welcomed me home. The incense she constantly burned no longer masked the stench of weed and homeliness. Martia stood by her bathroom door. She crossed her arms and tilted her head. She was pissed.

"What the fuck did you do, Aiden? Why. Are. You. Here. Looking like shit?" Her brown eyes were open wide with anger and disgust.

She took a hair tie she had on her wrist and tied her hair back into a ponytail. She looked like she was ready for a fight. I shook my head back and forth before glancing back at her, almost ashamed to be in her presence.

"I have nowhere else to go," my voice shook.

"How about your house, Aiden? Can't you ever just go to your fucking house? Did you even go to your house last night?"

"I... I can't. He was beating up my mom... I beat him up, Martia. I can't go back there."

"Jesus. Fucking. Christ, Aiden. What kind of a moron are you? Why can't you just let things happen? Your mom probably deserved to get beat. Why didn't you just leave like all the other times?" She stood in front of the bedroom door now, still with arms crossed, blocking my way out.

I sat on the bed, eyes on the floor, her words soaking into my brain. She always had a way with words. She always knew what to say. I held my tongue, trying to avoid a repeat of the previous night. I had never laid a finger on her, but anger always worked its way out.

"I can't keep fucking doing this, Martia. It has always been about the beatings, always the broken home. I honestly can't remember the last time I was happy... and that... that just sucks."

"You're a grown ass man, Aiden. You don't have to deal with that little kid shit anymore. But that doesn't mean you have to beat your old man and go to prison. You gotta think. Stop being so fucking emotional and think!"

She hit the side of her head, her eyes still big and still bulging.

She walked towards me, kicking her flip flops off.

"Get a real fucking job and move out. How are we supposed to start a family if you can't get your life right?"

34

"I can't deal with this. I can't deal with life right now."

I stood and limped past her towards the door.

"Stop being such a little bitch and do something!"

She stomped her leg on the floor. Trinkets on the dresser and nightstand shook. Some fell to the floor.

"Jesus, sometimes I feel like I'm the man in this relationship, Aiden. Where are you going?"

She clapped her hands and then crossed her arms again. "Look around, I am the greatest good you'll ever get!"

I did. With my head still lowered, I looked around. The piles of clothes on the floor and hippy band posters on the walls were my life. This was my greatest good.

"I have to get to work."

"Work? Oh my God... if you won't go to your house, you can't go out looking like that. My neighbors already think you're a fucking hobo, now they're gonna think you're also a rapist. A drunken rapist. You can't even walk straight. Come here... do a line. Then take a shower. You can borrow some of my dad's clothes."

She cut some lines on the dresser with her dad's credit card. She looked at me, patiently waiting. I leaned over and snorted. The white powder flew up my nose and opened my eyes wide. My body regained its strength and within seconds, euphoria took over.

"Atta boy. Now come here," she motioned me with her finger.

She pushed me onto the bed and pulled my jeans off. She grabbed my dick and swallowed it whole. Within seconds, it grew too big for the tight space. She pulled it out and wiped her mouth. She stared at me with intense desire. I smacked her across the face knocking her to the floor. She moaned, then laughed. I yanked her shorts off and threw them across the room. Her sweet white ass exposed my weakness. She knew I couldn't say no, I knew I had no choice. Those choices were always made for me. I went in raw like every other time, no concerns, no second thoughts.

I grabbed her ponytail and wrapped it around my wrist. I pulled back as I rammed her harder and harder. My balls smacked her, pleasure and pain pulsated throughout my body. As I neared explosion, I remembered my scene in the ditch by the reservoir. I remembered the semen of a strange man wrapping around my dick making me feel guilty and dirty. That also made me harder.

I wanted that semen to carry a deadly virus, one that would make her sick and miserable while putting me out of my own misery. The sick bitch deserved a Class A death, and I wanted to give it to her.

Thick globs of cum filled her before I pulled out and finished on her arched back. The white gel pooled at her butterfly tattoo. She trembled while she squirted at me, soaking my legs with a mixture of our fluids. I fell back onto the floor hard. Tears pushed through my lids and streamed down to my ears. This was my greatest good.

"Fucking hell, Aiden. Did you cum in me?! She slipped a couple fingers inside before pulling them out and staring at them.

"How many times do I have to tell you not to cum inside me?!"

She stood and ran to the bathroom holding her pussy. A few minutes later I heard the shower come on.

"Are you coming in?" she screamed out.

Chapter 5

I managed to get to work on time that morning.

I stood in the breakroom, staring at the schedule. The TV was loudly playing Spin the Wheel. The crowd cheered and the host made cheesy jokes. It was unnecessarily noisy. Every one of my problems danced around my head, mocking my misery.

I was stuck in a job I didn't like, living a life I didn't want. This life was a puzzle from which too many pieces were missing. I was a sick freak weirdo son of a bitch and didn't know why. My girlfriend hated me but refused to leave me and just a few hours prior I had either given her a deadly virus or an unwanted pregnancy.

Fuck. That's the last thing I needed. A kid would have simply made my life worse. Everybody thinks kids will make everything better. Couples on the brink of separation use them to try to make it work. In reality, they're just creating more broken people. This fucking world was already full of emotionally damaged fucks, we didn't need any more.

I was stuck with no way out, no way of making things right because I had no idea what right was. Every day was the same; just one regret after another. One fucking mistake after the other.

But how long could a fucked up man live before willingly giving up on himself? Every hour of my miserable life was spent fretting about everything that made me unhappy. There was no way out.

I went out to the floor and started to work. I arranged the same shelve for hours, pretending every book was one of my problems. No matter how I arranged them, I wasn't happy with the outcome. There was no solution.

Just as I was about to start over again, I noticed him staring at me out of the corner of my eye. It was that guy... Jesus, emo boy, Matte, whatever his name was.

He looked at me without hesitation. Even after I stared back, he didn't look away. I stared down at my borrowed green polo and khaki corduroy pants, then back at him. Still glaring... I looked around, and nobody else seemed to notice me, what a surprise.

I ignored him, went on to a different shelf, and began moving books. I moved some from the bottom shelf to the top shelf completely disregarding the correct process. Melvil Dewey could go fuck himself. I just needed to look busy. The last thing I needed was Malinda ratting me out to Mrs. Robinson.

Every single time I had gotten in trouble had been because of her incessant need for acquiesce. I don't know why she had to be that way. She was already perfect, blonde, hot, young, smart, and good at everything she tried her hands on. Why did she have to be such a nark? Mrs. Robinson would be completely oblivious to my lack of performance otherwise.

I was lost in thought before noticing him staring at me again. There was something mysterious about the way he stared. His eyes fixated on my face as if he was trying to read my mind. He pushed back his glasses and scratched the back of his head. No way was this guy good at his job either. Not with that lack of focus.

He moved up and down the aisle, moving books from the cart to the shelves. His hands moved without him even looking at them. They were almost robotic. But he didn't look at the covers or the numerical assignment. His eyes were stuck on me.

After a while, I realized I was staring at him, too. But it wasn't a normal stare. No, I was enchanted by this guy. I liked the way his straight hair covered his right eye and softly grazed his face. His lips moved gently, almost as if he recited lyrics to my favorite songs. I liked their natural pinkish red tone. I liked the way he ran his hand through his hair and left it messy, as if he didn't care how it looked.

I loved the tightness of his shirt and the way it raised a little when he moved his arms up. The action flashed a glimpse of skin that I would otherwise not see. My face burned a little every time.

But why, why was I doing that? Why was I watching him? Why did I like those things about him?

I shook my head, trying to gather myself. I looked up at the clock. Malinda had swapped it out again. She had taken down the bright sun shaped one and replaced it with an Abbott High panther face. I guess graduation season would soon be upon us. I hated her abundant support of education. Ugh, good thing my shift would be over in three minutes.

Three minutes?

I had watched the emo boy off and on for hours. He somehow managed to push away all my thoughts and made me think of only him. I glanced back at the shelves he had been arranging to catch one last glimpse before noticing he was gone. I looked around and spotted him walking towards the men's room by the front entrance.

Hurriedly, I went to the breakroom and grabbed my stuff out of my locker. I took one deep breath and walked out the front door. Yes, the front door. I had found my new drug.

I can't really understand why I did what I did the way I did it. It was as if for once in my life I took control and through all the bumps and holes on the road, I went after what I thought was good for me.

I mean, I needed friends, right? This guy appeared to be around my age. Judging by his style and music taste, he seemed cool. Maybe we could hang out sometime. What was the worst that could happen?

I stood by the door eagerly waiting. I wasn't too close that it seemed creepy, but close enough to catch him before he disappeared into the parking lot.

I placed one earphone in my ear and pressed "play" on the music app in my phone. "It's Almost Easy" began to blast. I waited and waited; the seconds dragging, allowing me to change my mind and change it all over again.

Malinda walked out, all happy and shit.

"Bye Aiden," she waved.

Ugh, shut up.

My stomach was uneasy, and my entire body trembled. The front door opened, and time slowed to a crawl. He stepped out and took a deep breath. He walked past me without even noticing my awkward presence. I stood frozen, watching the distance between us grow. Without my consent, my legs moved and followed him.

"Hey," I blurted out.

He turned and half smiled. "Hey, what's up?"

We were now face-to-face. His fresh and citrusy scent embraced me. It was almost like being young again, like sitting behind a shy guy in math class, like not being able to get enough of it. I was so close I could almost feel his body heat on me. My guts twisted and turned with nervousness.

"Nothing much," I replied.

"What you listening to?"

I remembered I was listening to music. I looked down at my phone and read the artist name to him.

"Avenged."

"Cool, I like them. You need a ride?" He looked around, probably trying to make sense of why I had stopped him.

"No, I'm good. Thanks."

"Alright. Well... I'll see you around then." He tapped my arm before turning to walk away.

It was now or never.

"Hey!" I called out louder than I needed to grab his attention.

He looked back, putting in an earphone.

My heart was at my throat, making it difficult for me to speak.

"Can... can I get your number?" I blurted out.

He smiled as the wind blew his fringe off his face, allowing me to see it completely for the first time. He had black eyes.

I gasped silently.

"Sure."

He recited the numbers, and I typed them into my phone with shaky fingers.

"I'm Aiden by the way." I looked up to meet his eyes.

"I know. We've met." He smiled again.

"Oh, yeah, sorry. I'm stupid." I shook my head.

Embarrassed, I turned and walked the other way, staring at his number displayed on my phone screen.

"I'm Matte, by the way."

I glanced back and let out a nervous laugh. I shook my head and continued to walk. My heart pounded away. It made me feel so good. It made me feel alive, and I wanted more. I opened my messages and typed a message.

"This is my number…" I wrote.

Not five seconds later he replied, "Cool. So, what's up?"

Chapter 6

The walk to my house was an unexpected breeze.

Every step became easier and easier. Strangers didn't stare and judge, and there were no stops or detours to do obscene acts beyond my control. For once, my head wasn't a jumbled mess of obsessive thoughts and repressed memories. I wasn't a fucked up guy from the lower valley anymore.

I was alive.

Every time my phone buzzed, I felt a little closer to being *normal* or at least a little less weird. I was on somebody's mind. I fucking mattered!

After the initial awkwardness of reintroducing myself, the conversation flowed smoothly. He laughed at the fact that I hadn't recorded his name in my memory in spite of working together for months and being formally introduced by Mrs. Robinson. Embarrassed, I kept apologizing over and over. He stated there was no need for apologies; that he understood. He said he always thought something was off about me, which was why he... liked me.

There it was again... Was it normal for a guy to *like* certain things about another guy?

I ignored the statement and swayed our conversation towards more relatable topics. I talked about music, and he rebounded talking about literature. He loved books and history. He loved learning, expanding his mind, and absorbing as much of the world as he could. Books took him to different worlds inside other people's minds the way music took me into their hearts. I liked that about *us*. How words connected us in similarly different ways.

He wanted to be a teacher: History or English. He wasn't sure yet. He was taking a year off college to get to meet people and learn their stories. He wanted to know what purpose they thought they had in life. He wanted to know what moved them and what stopped them. It was a social experiment, or at least that's what he called it.

It wasn't long before he tried to dig personal items out of my head. He asked about my past... what high school I'd graduated from, previous jobs, ex-girlfriends, my birthday.

"I went to West High School, the library is kinda my first job, I hate all my exes, and my birthday is June 21," I texted.

I answered his questions with short responses, refusing to let him dig deeper. The less he knew about me, the better chance I had to be someone else, someone he would like and accept.

"What about you?" I wanted to know everything about him.

"Well, I moved a lot as a kid. I graduated from Abbott High School though. My first job was at the movies, Western World. My exes are cool and my birthday was last week, May 4th.

I texted him just as he texted me, "How old are you?"

"LOL, I just turned twenty-one. You?" he said.

"Lol, I'll be twenty-two," I said.

"Sweet. We should try to con Mrs. Robinson into buying us a cake lol."

"Lol."

Now standing in the dark front yard of my house, my mind wandered off. I thought about the many times I witnessed my father's efforts to destroy it. I thought about the threats recorded on the walls. His toxic words filled the entire place with an illness that made the air stale. My mother's tears rotted holes on everything they touched. Her sighs and cries were the ghosts that lingered above our heads when we tried to sleep at night. Every inch of that house was tainted with tales of their *obviously* successful marriage and the family they had created out of guilt and mistakes.

Nothing had *lived* there in years.

I thought about my brother, the only light in that pit. Despite everything, he always appeared happy. I tried so hard to keep him oblivious to his rapidly decaying family. I thought about the many sleepless nights I spent cradling him from birth, painting happy pictures in his head about worlds that existed in my drugs.

What held that house together? It was never a home, and it would never be one. All the pieces to that puzzle lay strewn on the very ground I stood on. Some were even lost, perhaps forever.

My phone continued to buzz, snapping me back to reality. It had never pulsated with so much life before. I pulled it out of my pocket and read his messages. Each letter of his words rebuilt a tiny part of my decomposing world. They shed light around my house when there was nothing there to power it. Matte was establishing himself as the nightlight in the darkness of my life.

I went inside and walked the dark halls to my room. Usually by the time I went to bed, I was already tripping out, diving into the made-up worlds that kept me alive. But tonight was different. I lay on my bed and let him distract me from all that broke me. I allowed his words to cradle the child inside me that never got the chance to grow up. I felt like I had a chance for change.

For the first time since I could remember, I fell asleep completely sober.

The next morning, I awoke to eighteen unread messages, three from Martia and fifteen from Matte. The warm fuzzy feeling others had described invaded my body and distracted me from the pain. I needed a hit of something to make it through the day. I ignored Martia's messages and tapped on Matte's. As I read about his night, I envisioned myself with him.

We sat on his bed as he told me about a book he was reading, Apocalyptic Love. I'd have to look it up. I plodded at his side as we went to the kitchen and got a snack. We listened to the songs I sent him before falling asleep. We picked out clothes for the next morning and showered before going to bed. Together we were slowly building our own little world, one word at a time.

I replied ecstatically to his texts and asked him what he thought about the songs I had sent. His immediate response was the hit that would get me through the day.

"I loved them. I especially liked Don't Wait," he texted.

That was my favorite, too.

I got up and stepped out my bedroom. The grey halls of my house lit up as I walked them. My colorless world became pigmented with his words. I took a shower and brushed my teeth. I

44

tried to comb my hair but I had no style. It lay flat to one side. At least it wasn't all over the place like it usually was.

My mother had taped a note to the front door. "Your father is in jail," was all she wrote. There was no sign of her or my brother. Like usual, they were gone before I started my day.

Mrs. Robinson had asked us to work for a few hours extra that Saturday. It was odd but I was OK with it, only so I could see Matte. When I entered the library, I spotted him arranging books in the fiction section. He wore a purple t-shirt with bright yellow letters on the front that read "I partied naked with Bruised Horizons." The band t-shirt went perfect with his faded blue jeans. The man had impeccable style. It was great to see him and to know that little bit of him lived inside my pocket.

I waved at him. The act made me feel weird. I pulled my hand back and stuffed it in my pocket.

He waved back, giving me a half smile.

"Thank you for coming in today, Aiden. I really do appreciate that. Could you please man the main counter today?" Mrs. Robinson appeared behind me.

"Um, yeah sure."

I hated the main counter, but today I was actually excited about it. I left my stuff in my locker and headed out. My phone buzzed in my pocket every few minutes, reminding me Matte was still thinking about me. I saw him in the distance, checking his phone and looking at me every time he said something funny.

It was insane to think that just twenty-four hours ago, we were no more than puppets at the same show. Somehow, by an act of randomness, our strings crossed, and now we were tangled; the more we moved and talked, the closer we became.

"Why are you all giddy today?" Malinda asked.

I hadn't even noticed she was sitting in the chair next to me. I shrugged and smiled then looked at my phone again.

"Stop it, I don't like it." She sounded completely disgusted with me.

The day went by faster than I could manage. I tried to enjoy every minute, savoring every word, every second. Malinda shot her eyes at me angrily every time I got a text, but I ignored her. After a while, I felt like she was about to rat me out, when out of nowhere

Mrs. Robinson tripped on the cart she was bringing in from outside.

Instantly, people gathered around her concerned. An older man helped her up and a young lady helped her to the chairs in the main entry way.

I looked over to Matte. Seeing him trying to hold his laughter made me burst out laughing. Shocked patrons shot me the stink eye as I ran towards the men's room to finish my outburst.

At the end of my shift I lingered in the break room, waiting nervously for him. My heart pounded heavily, I felt its beat on my fingertips as I gripped my phone in my hands. Malinda came and went. She tried talking to me but I ignored her. The minutes ticked and fell off the face of the clock. The door swung open, and he walked in. Both our faces lit up the second our eyes met.

"Hey, what you up to?" he asked.

"Nothing much, just grabbing my stuff. You?"

"Same. Dude, wasn't it funny when Mrs. Robinson tripped on the cart today?" He held his stomach as he laughed.

"Yeah, hahaha, books went everywhere." I looked down, trying to hide my smile with my hand.

I hated my smile. It made my cheeks look big.

"All these old ladies can't keep tripping or else we'll have no employees!"

We laughed and poked fun at Mrs. Robinson's clumsy ass. I looked at him enjoying himself. I liked how his hair naturally fell over his glasses, partially hiding his eyes. I liked the way he laughed and walked as he recreated the hilarious event. I liked how his shirt lifted up revealing a little bit of his abdomen every time he raised his arms. I liked his style and the way he moved with confidence.

"Alright man, I gotta go." He gave me a double thumbs up.

"Oh... OK."

I didn't want it to be over. I wanted to go with him and hang out at his house... maybe even his room. Something inside me wanted more and I couldn't understand why.

"I'll text you later." He smiled and walked away.

"Alright." I smiled back.

And he was gone. Just like that. I missed him already. God damn it! I missed him. I felt so empty without him.

I walked out the break room and out the front door again. I even said goodbye to Mrs. Robinson. I wasn't sure how I felt about that yet. As I walked across the parking lot, my phone buzzed again.

"Don't trip on your way out, lol," Matte said.

"LOL," I replied.

What was happening to me? No one had ever made me feel the way Matte did. No exes, no friends, no one. The last time I trusted someone enough to call friend, I was a child. Things were different, people change as they grow older. Matte was different. He was confident, smart, funny, and… cute.

I shook my head at the thought. What was I thinking? It wasn't right, I couldn't be attracted to him. He was a guy. I couldn't be attracted to a guy. Could I? It was wrong… but was it?

My hands clenched into fists tightly. Why? Why was this happening to me? Why was it wrong? Why did it feel so right? Why?

I broke my trance and looked up only to realize I stood in my front yard. The darkness returned. Before my mind could process it, Martia rolled up in her beater. She parked beside me. The dust that followed her surrounded us. She stepped out and stomped towards me, furious.

"I waited for you yesterday and today and you never came out. Why the fuck haven't you answered any of my texts? And all my calls? They go straight to voicemail." She threw her hands in the air. "Answer ME!"

I couldn't. My head was still dancing with my heart.

"What the fuck is wrong with you, Aiden?" Martia asked again, this time tapping the side of my head.

I held my phone in my hand as it buzzed away. Without thinking about it, I looked at the new message. It was Matte asking about the last concert I had attended. I smiled and started to reply. Martia slapped the phone out of my hand, pulling the earphones out of my ears as it fell to the ground.

"I see your phone works fine." Martia stood with her arms across her chest.

"Fuck off, Martia."

"What? What did you just say to me?"

47

"FUCK! OFF! Get out of my fucking face, Martia. Do you understand that?!"

"Oh look at you, so angry."

"Fuck you, get out of here! I don't want to see you ever again. Don't you get that? I thought you were smarter than me. You always gloat about that."

She was shocked. She had never seen me defend myself. But it was the only way she would understand. For once in my life, I had something I wanted, and I would not allow her to get in the way.

She took a step back and searched for words.

"You know what? Whatever, Aiden. I'm the best thing you've got. The best you'll ever have. Your house is a dump, your brother is a retard, your dad is a drunk, your mom is a pushover idiot, and you… oh, sweetheart, you are the worst of the bunch. You are nothing but a pathetic, pussy ass junkie. Your entire life is garbage. You can kiss this ass goodbye."

"You're right, your life is so much better than mine, Martia. I'm sorry it has to be like this. Stay safe."

I picked up my phone and turned the screen on. Cracks spider-webbed down from the top right corner of the screen. I dragged my steps into my house. She wasn't worth the argument. That relationship had died the moment Matte came into my life.

"Fuck you, faggot! Faggot! Faggot!"

I heard her screaming my name as I made my way to my room. Through the cracks on my phone screen, I read Matte's new messages. Through every one of them, I saw Matte's evening deteriorating.

"Man, I'm signing off for a little bit. I need to think…" his last message read.

I didn't want him to go but at the same time, I didn't know how to make him stay.

"I feel you… sometimes it helps to be completely alone," I replied.

Now I was completely alone.

I didn't hear from him all day Sunday. On Monday morning I woke up again to no new messages. The emptiness spread from my phone to the coffin I called home. Everything felt dead again. I rubbed the newly formed cracks on my phone and got ready for work.

The library was emptier than usual, no hipsters or college students. Mrs. Robinson was in her office, alone. Malinda was off and Matte was nowhere to be seen. I left my stuff in my locker and reported to my station. Today, I was to arrange magazines. We had a new shipment, so I was to display the newer ones and discard the older ones.

I opened the boxes and lay everything in piles on the floor around me. A couple people walked by giving me quizzing looks and skipping over my piles. I'm sure my system only made sense to me.

"Sorry," I said.

The lady frowned and walked away fast. Her teenage son "'sup" nodded me and I "'sup" nodded back. It was a stupid gesture, but it was something guys did to acknowledge presence.

I checked my phone after every couple magazines, hoping to see Matte's name displayed through the cracks. But there was nothing. My stomach started to hurt but I continued working.

When I got to last month's sports magazine, I noticed something off. The magazine was stiffer than the rest. I rubbed my fingers on the ridges bulging out on the front cover and knew exactly what was happening. I flipped through the pages until I found a cluster stuck together. I pulled it up to my face and the familiar scent of semen stung my nose. I looked around before ripping the pages off and placing them in my back pocket. The act sickened me, but the company would help me feel less lonely.

Martia was right, I was a loser and... perhaps a faggot. I had nothing in my life, and I couldn't get Matte out of my head. I couldn't understand why he was so ingrained in every fiber of my mind. It happened so fast. I was immediately obsessed with him.

I guess that's how infatuation works. When you've had nothing your entire life, the second anything good comes across... you become obsessed. And the more you get, the more you want. But at some point, the more you want, the less you'll get.

I looked at my phone again. It was noon. I hadn't heard from him since Saturday night. I stood up and glanced around for him. Aside from a few people by the audiobooks and a mom with her baby carriage, no one else was around.

I checked the parking lot, maybe he was running late. I tripped on my way back inside and scraped my hand on the sidewalk. I went to the men's room to wash my hand and checked to see if he was there. Nothing. The breakroom yielded no results either. I even searched in Mrs. Robinson's office. My head was pounding.

After looking in the computer room, I found him. He was sitting alone at the farthest corner of the library, where people went to think. That corner was like a magnet for those who craved solitude. The large windows framed the outside world perfectly encapsulating winter regardless of the season, showing us how dead West was.

I often saw high school graduates sitting there, pondering days before and days after their graduations. They had no idea where life would take them. I saw young women dreaming about what their lives would have been if they hadn't had the kids that played nearby. Their overpriced coffee drinks and fashion magazines gave them away.

That was where I decided to take the job a few years back.

I knew Matte had something on his mind, perhaps something that he didn't want to share. I didn't want to disturb him but at the same time, I knew we both needed each other. As I approached him he looked up and smiled. He took one earphone out and said, "Sit... here, be emo with me." He handed me the earphone as I took a seat next to him.

There, on that sofa, I was so close to him. Closer than I had ever been. I longed for that moment since we started talking. I never expected it would happen as it did, but it was better than I could ever imagine.

I couldn't stop wondering what was wrong. Something was off; I could feel it in the air. He was close but distant. He smiled, but inside he shattered.

"Is... everything OK?" I asked already knowing the answer.

He looked over at me and simply smiled.

"Is... there something I can do?" I wanted to know, and I wanted to help him be him again.

He sighed. "Yes, I just need you here with me. Just be here and listen to music with me."

I put the earphone in my ear and listened as music and lyrics trickled in. The song was slow, and the singer's voice unique. He was in pain like we were. He sang of betrayal, recounting to someone special how he felt. He wanted that person to know what she meant to him and how much it hurt when she cheated on him. He wanted us to know that he wished they would've never met. All the pain could have been avoided if they had simply never met. The best deceptions are always hidden in plain sight.

I felt the words. I felt the pain. I felt Matte's knee touching mine… I felt the warmth expanding from his knee to my heart.

I thought about moving it but waited to see if he would and when he didn't, neither did I.

And as the song came to an end, that moment in time was officially recorded in my head for the rest of eternity.

Chapter 7

Matte and I worked together the rest of the day. Not even our assigned duties could pull us apart.

We walked out together to collect the books from the drop box. He spun the lock on his finger as I wheeled the cart out. I reminded him of the time someone threw shredded porn in the drop box. It was singlehandedly the most embarrassing moment of my life. We pushed the cart inside together recounting our side of the story to each other.

"I was so embarrassed. I didn't know what to do. So I just bolted."

"Dude, I just remembered seeing you run to the restroom leaving behind a trail of books."

"I didn't care, I just wanted to hide."

"You wanna know a secret?"

He had a mischievous look on his face.

"Umm... sure."

"My friend did that. He thought it was gonna be me pulling the cart inside that day."

"Shut up!"

"Dude, I'm serious."

"Fuck!"

"I know, I'm sorry man!"

I pressed my lips and shook my head, my cheeks burning red. I looked at him laughing, genuinely enjoying himself.

"Fuck, Mrs. Robinson will be pissed we're both out here," he said jumping out of view from the glass door.

I saw Mrs. Robinson walking around aimlessly inside. Matte had a point. She'd be pissed if we both walked inside, wheeling the cart together.

Fearing she'd catch us, Matte went ahead of me to cause a distraction so I could make it past unnoticed. I held back my laugh as he stumbled around in her office. He tripped on her trash bin and knocked a stack of papers from her desk. Mrs. Robinson struggled to get him up off the floor.

He was such a goofball.

I pushed the cart inside and left it by the main counter, ready to be scanned in. Matte joined me a few minutes later. I helped him log the books back into the system instead of reporting back to my assigned station. I grabbed the books and passed them to him. He scanned their barcodes and threw them on a different cart. Our fingers touched every time he took a book from me. I couldn't hold my smile.

We took the scanned book cart and started cataloging the books on shelves. We were so close together, we bumped shoulders a couple of times. It made no sense, but we burst out laughing and giggling like schoolboys. He put his arm on my shoulders and tried to catch his breath. I put my arm around his waist and tried to keep my heart in my chest.

We separated in unison and stood there for a few seconds. I stared at his face; his hair, his jawline, his lips and followed his eyes as they traced my face and locked on my lips. We were trapped in each other's pull and nothing else mattered. No one else existed.

I still felt his warmth on my leg. It expanded upwards to my heart making it skip beats. My stomach filled with bubbles that traveled to my head. My breath escaped my body to mingle with his.

"Hey, so you don't drive here, huh?"

The question brought me back to Earth.

"No, I walk every day."

"That's crazy. Like, every day?"

"Yeah. I like walking."

"You like walking…" He smiled, nodding. "That's cool. You feel like walking today?"

Where was he going with this?

"Umm, kinda?"

He laughed.

"Dude, I'm trying to give you a ride tonight."

53

My stomach dropped to the floor and my arms went numb. He wanted to drive me to my house? I didn't want him to know where I lived. I didn't want him to see the shithole I crawled out of every day.

"Umm, no it's OK. You don't have to."

"Dude, I know I don't have to. I just wanna waste some time with you."

My cheeks burned.

He wanted us to hang out. I wiped the sweat off my forehead and thought about it for a moment. This was what I'd been desperately longing for since the day we met. I had imagined myself by his side at work, in his car, at his house. It was the natural progression of things. I had to give in.

"OK, sure if you insist."

I wanted to spend the rest of eternity in his presence, with his knee touching mine and his arm around me like I was his and he was mine!

"Alright. It's a date." He smiled.

A date? Like a date date?

My breath finally escaped my lungs entirely, taking my heart with it. They danced in slow motion around me. They jumped on my head and pulled at my hair. This was it. This was the next step in our friendship!

I couldn't think clearly the rest of the day. My head floated away with thoughts that both made me happy and nervous at the same time. The closer the clock ticked to 7 p.m., the more intense everything got.

After I finished displaying all the new magazines, I decided to help cataloguing. Matte shelved books across from me. Every time our eyes locked, I dropped half the shelf. When I went to pick them up, I couldn't find their location as the titles kept shape-shifting. I swear they kept trying to tell me something!

"Matte... date...date... Matte... date Matte... Date Date Matte!... DATE MATTE!"

I was sweating profusely in every area of my body, my eyes pulsated with my heartbeat, and my throat was dry and rough.

I shook my head trying to make everything return to normal. But I couldn't get the imagery of a date with Matte out of my brain.

"You ready?" Matte bumped me with his shoulder. It was 7 p.m.

I looked at the panther face clock. *Fucking Malinda.*

"Umm, yeah, let me get my stuff." I tried to hold my grin.

"OK, I'll meet you outside."

I grabbed my stuff as quickly as I could. Each minute spent with myself was a minute spent without him. I stormed out the front door and spotted him standing where I once waited for him. Time halted and allowed me to record the moment into my brain. I counted my steps as I walked up to him, five... six... seven... eight, dragging each one to savor it all.

He stood as a burning silhouette against the setting sun. Cicadas clicked away and cactus wren challenged them. The dry breeze swept his fresh, sweaty, citrusy scent onto me, recounting the day and encapsulating the moment. I melted on the scorching sidewalk.

He scrolled on his phone. His thumb moved slowly up and up, then down, then up again until he saw me approaching. He slid the phone in his pocket and took a few steps towards me. He gazed at me from my feet to my face, his eyes searching for reasons to smile.

Every time I think of summer, I think of that moment.

We walked together to his car. The parking lot was empty except for two cars, Mrs. Robinson's and his tiny gray sports car. He unlocked it and we climbed in.

I looked around the cabin taking it in. His car was immaculate. I couldn't find a speck of filth on it. No empty water bottles or candy wrappers. No piles of clothes or backpacks in the back seat, nothing.

He put the key in the ignition and turned it on. The extra keys on the ring dangled back and forth crashing with the purple steel clip. We sat for a moment. Music played through the speakers barely audible. Matte sat quietly, tapping his hands on the steering wheel. The veins on his forearms were so pronounced. I stared at them for a second as he continued to tap. In the short time I knew him, I had never seen him so quiet.

"You OK?" I asked.

Matte remained silent for a second, looking ahead.

"Yeah, just shit at home. That's all. I think I'll need to move out soon. But don't worry about me." He glanced back at me, his head cocked to one side. "Are you OK?"

Was I? I was with him, but that was superficial. Being around him made me happy but didn't erase everything I'd lived through. So, I guess I wasn't? But I couldn't tell him that. It was too soon to send him running for the hills.

"I think so." I wondered if he'd believe me.

He nodded.

"Don't take this the wrong way, man, I just feel like sometimes you're lost in your head. We worked together for months, and you didn't even know I existed."

I looked at my feet embarrassed.

"Yeah… I just like to think."

"Dude, no one likes to think. People only think whenever there's something wrong."

My whole life was wrong.

I sighed.

"I didn't mean to push. I just want you to know that you can talk to me if you aren't."

I guess he didn't believe me.

He squeezed my shoulder and said, "Alright, guide me!"

I gave him directions to my house. He put the car in drive, and we sped off.

My house wasn't too far from the library. It was a shame. I would have liked to drive with him for hours. I wanted to tell him to drive off into the distance on the highway. I wanted to tell him to take me to get some tacos or get slushies. But I didn't. I sat quietly and looked out the window at scenery dashing by.

How could I make him aware that he was already helping me? I didn't need to talk. I simply needed to be with him.

The song we listened to in the library came up in the shuffle. He put the volume up as it started. He tapped the steering wheel to the tempo and silently sang the words. He closed his eyes briefly as the singer delivered the chorus.

I listened to the lyrics carefully trying to memorize them.

"We said forever,
But you thought forever was too long.

I said baby, 'let's keep trying,'
And now you're gone.

You were my whole world,
Even when you weren't.
I lost my whole world,
When I saw you in his arms."
Such strong words.

Every song that came up on the shuffle was perfect. You can really learn a lot from someone by the music they listen to. Matte was in distress. His favorite song depicted betrayal and yearned for self-healing. Something major had to have happened. But what?

"This is my house. The one on the right."

My house was a three bedroom box my father built with the help of his addict friends. The windows were small, and the doors sat crooked. It stood out in the neighborhood as it sat for decades without paint or curb appeal. It was my prison.

We stopped on the curb right in front. I didn't want it to be over. I wasn't even out of the car yet and I already felt time pulling us apart. He turned the music down and looked past me at my house. I clenched my teeth as I exposed the source of my misfortune.

I looked over my shoulder to see the image Matte saw. The patchy grass and rusted fence greeted us. My father's truck and mother's car sat lonely in the driveway. A shadow moved behind the living room curtains. Signs of life, I suppose. The house wasn't completely dead.

"I should go inside. I'm kinda hungry."

Matte sat back on his seat and tapped on the steering wheel with drumstick fingers.

"OK"

"Well, thanks for the ride."

"No problem. Thank you for the company. Maybe next time we can get some ice cream or something."

I pressed my lips and nodded in agreement.

I stepped out into the hot air and gently shut the door. I stood on the sidewalk and watched Matte drive off. I glared at my house and dreaded going in. The stale air depressed me, drove me to insanity. It wasn't a house. It wasn't a home. Who I was with Matte didn't like who I was in my own personal hell.

My feet dragged as I made my way to the front door. The cracks on the driveway ran in the opposite direction trying to escape. I couldn't even think of all the times I had tried to do the same. I grabbed the doorknob and my mind raced to every instance I found the aftermath of a fight. My mom on the floor covered in blood, bruises, cuts, sometimes even unconsciousness.

Why didn't she fight back? Why was it so hard for her to fight back, just one time? That's all it would've taken for that bastard to get it. What was she so afraid of?

As I opened the door, I got a message from Matte. I tapped on it, and the link sent me to our song: "The Best Times" by Unspoken Confessions.

That night, I lay on the roof of my house staring at the sparkled sky. I played our song on my phone over and over again, reliving that moment in my head. I felt Matte's warmth embracing me, making my blood tingle. Every text from him filled my stomach with bubbles and lifted the demons away from me. I was happy.

For the first time in my life, I was genuinely happy.

"I'm really glad we got to hang out," he texted.

"Me too," I replied.

"Hey, I don't want to keep pushing, but I really want you to know you can count on me whenever :)" he said.

"Thanks :)" I replied.

The confusion secreted by my brain started popping every bubble in my stomach. I couldn't understand what was happening. What was this? Was I in love? Was that what the *word* felt like? My head was a mess, and my heart ached for more.

A thunderstorm rumbled in the distance. The approaching breeze was cool, and the smell of rain caressed me. It brought back memories of growing up. I remembered running from my problems and the people that hurt me. I remembered suppressing the feelings that came naturally to me. I couldn't be gay. I refused to.

I remembered lying on the roundabout in the playground as the night fell. I spun around looking up at the lightning above me. It scattered through the darkened skies, showing me the different

58

pathways of life. I thought about the future. I fantasized about being happy. Who would hold me in their arms and put me back together? Who would show me how to... love?

It felt like ages ago.

I sat up and rested my head on my knees. I wanted him so badly. My soul stretched out from my body and pulled at the distance between us. It left my body empty, waiting to be filled by his return. I wanted to be with him more than I had ever wanted anything.

I looked down at my leg. Our knees touching was just the beginning. Him consciously not moving away was the next move. He accepted me, even if it was just as a friend, he had already accepted me. It was a clusterfuck of emotions, and my thoughts choked on him.

Across town lights went out. Soon the world around me would be asleep, and I would be alone with the storm brewing within me. People would sleep tight with the falling rain cradling them as they floated away in their dreams. In the waking world, I fought for my dream to become a reality.

Chapter 8

Over the next five weeks, Matte and I continued to waste time with each other. We spent days at the library together, working, talking, and making each other laugh. He brought out the best of me. I didn't even recognize the person I was with him. I cracked jokes, I told him about things that I found interesting and things that drove me crazy. Or should I say the people that drove me crazy?

I told him about the day Malinda started to work at the library, a year after me. I knew the second I saw her interact with Mrs. Robinson, she would be my greatest nemesis. I disagreed with her ass-kissing and her striving to be the perfect employee.

"You didn't think she was kinda hot?"

"Malinda? I guess for a few seconds before she opened her mouth."

Matte laughed hysterically at my comeback and undeniable reasoning.

"I can't say I don't see what you mean," Matte said between gasps for air.

I couldn't help but wonder if he thought she was hot. If anyone could get on her level, it was him. As much as I wanted to know, I didn't ask. I guess I didn't really want to know his answer. I didn't know what I would do if he said he was attracted to her. Although, I only saw them interact a handful of times. For all I knew, he could've had a crush on her.

The thought made me a little jealous.

Those five weeks felt like a dream come true. Matte and I had become nearly inseparable. Our days were filled with each other, each one better than the last. And when we parted for the night, we kept each other company through our texts. It was almost as if we lived in each other's pockets, in each other's minds, exactly where we wanted each other to be.

Fact is, I knew I was *different* long before I met Matte. I always felt like I wasn't meant to follow the social standards. I felt that I liked guys more than I did girls. But those thoughts were pushed to the back of my mind by the people who surrounded me. Or the people that abused me I should say. They dictated a large portion of my life.

Now, I was a grown man. Now, I could make my own choices. Now, I could *love* who I wanted to love.

One day right before our shift was over, Mrs. Robinson called Matte to her office. We were both confused and nervous about the sudden meeting.

"What can she possibly want? Did she say anything else?"

"No, she just said she needed to see me before I left for the day."

"What if somebody complained about you? Or fucking Malinda said something."

"It's alright man, I'm sure it's nothing," he said before disappearing between the shelves.

I lingered in the break room a few minutes. The hands on the clock above the door circled. I walked around the couch biting my nails, wondering what was being said. I checked my phone over and over, waiting for a text from him. 7:05 p.m. came and went. 7:10 p.m. reminded me that it was almost dark out.

By 7:20 p.m., I could no longer wait. Walking in the desert at night wasn't a good idea. I collected my things and left the building. I looked back at the front door a few times, hoping he'd walked out. He didn't, and soon the library disappeared in the in the cold sandy ripples of the arroyo bed.

At 7:37 p.m. I felt my phone buzz in my pocket.

I pulled it out and read, "Where are you?"

My insides went cold, and I stood frozen. I looked towards the library and considered running back. The creepy rustling shrubbery fought my thoughts. I couldn't go back. It would be dark by the time I got there. And if he had already left, I would have to walk back in complete darkness.

"I left… sorry I didn't think you'd want me to wait for you," I texted back.

Silence.

I waited. The sun hid behind the horizon, and the coolness of the desert started to rise.

"I'm sorry man. I really didn't think about it. I just assumed you wouldn't mind," I tried again.

I waited. The clear skies sparkled above me. I could no longer distinguish shrubs from scary hallucinations. I couldn't stick around any longer. I began to walk again. My feet were heavy, and my steps dragged.

Just as I arrived home, my phone buzzed.

"No worries…" he said.

That dot dot dot after his words banged my head like a hammer. *No worries…*

Three seconds later, my phone buzzed again.

"I'll see you tomorrow."

Tomorrow?

My knees shook and my mind instantly flooded with thoughts and questions.

Was I wrong to leave? I was such an idiot, I should have waited. We always walked out together. For the last five weeks, we had walked out together every single night; of course, he wanted me to wait. I was such a fucking idiot. I didn't want him to be angry at me.

I went inside and straight to my room. I threw my stuff on the floor and rummaged through my nightstand drawers until I found it. I stared at the tin full of strips in my hand. They trembled as I tried to convince myself that I didn't need drugs.

Don't… don't…

"Fuck!"

I hadn't used drugs in weeks. I was already past the point where I needed them to live.

Just fucking do it already.

My phone buzzed again. I held my breath.

I closed the tin and dropped it in my drawer. I pulled the phone out of my pocket and stared at his words.

"But seriously, don't worry, man :)"

I exhaled. Air rushed through my lungs, relaxing my tense muscles.

The happy face after his words instantly calmed me down.

"Alright, see you tomorrow :)" My fingers trembled as I texted back.

The next morning, I woke up to eleven new messages, all from Matte. Anxiously, I unlocked my phone and tapped on his name. I read each word at least twice as I couldn't believe what he was saying.

He proposed we skipped work. It was barely Wednesday, and he wanted to skip work. That was such an irresponsible thing to do. That was such a Matte thing do.

"Why not go out and have fun?" he said.

I had never called off work, but the idea of spending the day with him and only him was irresistible.

"Yes! Let's do it!" I replied.

After a miserable attempt at convincing Mrs. Robinson I was ill, I was out the door. Matte picked me up in front of my house for the first time.

His car looked different, in broad daylight. Smaller, and a little more beat up. I hopped in and adjusted the seatbelt.

"Check it out!"

"Check what out?"

"Dude, c'mon. You seriously don't see it?"

I looked around the cab searching for something different.

"No, sorry."

"I got a little balloon dog air freshener." He pointed at the air vent.

I smiled and nodded.

I could tell Matte loved the car. He went on and on telling me how he got it and what he had fixed on it. His car was the main reason he got a full-time job. It was his baby.

I couldn't understand. I had never had any materialistic desires. But it was cute to see Matte excited about something so simple.

We drove around town for hours visiting places he frequented. Matte was really enthused to show me where he went to school and what jobs he'd had growing up.

We stopped by the movie theater West-ern World. It had been Matte's first job and apparently the best popcorn he'd ever eaten. We went by the concessions and grabbed a bucket before making our way to the arcade. I wondered why we didn't just watch a movie, but I didn't ask. It wasn't like any good movies were playing anyway.

Instead we walked around eating popcorn and watching others play. We took a few turns at the claw machine but didn't win anything. Matte talked to everyone we encountered. The conversations flowed naturally as if he'd known the people for years. It was the oddest thing, and it made me a little uncomfortable.

On our way out, Matte high-fived a couple guys working the ticket booth. They looked a little older than us. But they had the same alternative style as him. It was weird; he didn't seem like the type of person who'd high-five in public places. He kept surprising me more and more.

The theater was underwhelming. The popcorn was stale, and the arcade over-priced. But I was glad to see where Matte had spent many nights as a high school boy. I imagined him working and hanging out, saving the necessary money to buy his beloved car. The job held a special place in his heart. I got that. After years of working at the library, it too, now, held a special place in my heart.

I tried to picture myself around teenaged Matte, but I couldn't. We were part of two very different worlds. He was the type of guy that hung out in the parking lot after school and went to friend's houses to play video games on Friday nights. I was more like the type who ditched class to fuck and get high.

We were two very different people.

After the theater, we drove by a skate park at the opposite side of town. Matte slowed down and pointed at a half-pipe.

"See that?"

I nodded.

"That's where I had my fist kiss... fifth grade... Delilah." He grinned ear to ear.

I nodded and shrugged.

"She was cool. Turned lesbo freshman year. Although, I think she has a kid now."

The skate park made me want to vomit. It was all concrete, ramps, slopes, half-pipes, and of course, no shade. I couldn't even imagine spending five minutes out there. The sun was too much to handle, specially reflecting off the concrete. Especially in the summer. No thanks.

Why did Matte tell me about Delilah? What point did he have to make?

We drove by the mall, his elementary, middle, and high school. Each location, he told me about a different memorable moment like the time shoplifted some earrings from "Carol's" in the mall for his seventh-grade girlfriend. And the time he ate so much mac and cheese, he puked all over the gym during P.E. in third grade.

But I think my favorite story was the one when he ditched health class in tenth grade with his friend Mark. They hid in the boys locker-room for an entire afternoon. They talked about games, girls, shit at home, and their English teachers rack. When they got cold, they decided to turn on all the showers so the steam could warm them up. They got busted by the custodian before the school day was over.

I wondered if there was more to the story. It seemed a little odd that he and his friend were in there all alone for hours. Then they turned the showers on to "warm up?" I wanted to ask him if they showered. I wanted him to tell me they did something other than just talk.

My mind drifted for a few seconds. I imagined myself with him, hiding in the locker room. Just us two, alone, talking about teenage hormonal shit. I would've loved to spend time with him. Maybe even shower with him.

Why couldn't we have met back then?

The thought made me uneasy. Someone like him would've never hung out with someone like me.

Through every location I felt like he wanted me to know a different side of him. He showed me bits and pieces, trying to put together a slideshow of his life. It was perfect.

He talked and talked while I listened and listened. I didn't have much to say. Nothing exciting ever happened to me. And I couldn't find a way to say, "Hey, by the way, I'm a total fuck up, I was *abused* as a child, and I love doing drugs to escape my sad excuse of a life. I don't have any hobbies because I don't even want to be alive."

Those are the little things no one wants to hear.

Chapter 9

We stopped for pizza at lunch time. Matte wanted to try a new place that opened by the train station, Click's Pizza. I had never heard of the place.

When we pulled up, I was surprised to see the size of the establishment. It was big enough to hold at least a couple hundred people. With it being 1 p.m. on a Wednesday, the locale was nearly empty.

"How'd you hear of this place?" I asked.

"Oh, my brother applied for a job here a couple weeks ago. He said it looked pretty legit."

"Your brother?"

"Yeah. I've got two older brothers, twins actually, and a younger sister."

"Twins... wow."

"Yeah, that's what my mom told me my dad said when they found out. You'd think they'd stop there, haha. You've got any siblings?"

"I have a younger brother."

"Nice. So, you think a large pepperoni would be OK?"

"Umm, yeah, that's cool. I'm not too hungry."

Matte ordered the pizza while I stood behind by the doors. I couldn't help but stare at him from a distance. He looked so freaking cute; basic black T, washed out skinny jeans, and classic Chucks. Perfection.

I decided to look around to distract myself. The loud music and arcade games made me nauseous. This was not my scene. But at least it wasn't too crowded. That would've thrown me over the edge.

Forty-five minutes later, we sat across from each other with the pizza between us. Matte took a couple slices, and I took one. He ate so fast I couldn't keep up. I took a bite here and there when he wasn't looking. The fear of him thinking I chewed loudly or with my mouth open only made my stomach hurt more.

Matte told me more about his family as he waited for me to finish eating.

He was fortunate enough to have his mom taking care of the household. She had odd jobs throughout his childhood but for the most part, she was available to raise them. His dad had a good job as a plant manager for a prepared foods factory. It had taken him about fifteen years to get to that point, but he had done it. It was a complete contrast to my family.

Ambition and dedication didn't really tickle my father's fancy.

We walked around the arcade after our meal. Matte went on and on about some of the classic games they had. They reminded him of growing up with his brothers. I was terrible at every one we tried. I had never played video games. Getting the hang of the controls was nearly impossible.

After a while Matte got tired of winning. I get it, it's only fun if it's a challenge. He went off to take a leak while I tried my hand at Skee-ball. I sucked at it, too. After scoring only 100 points, I flipped the machine the middle finger.

"You look like you're ready to go, haha."

"Yeah." I scratched the back of my head, embarrassed.

"So where do you want to go now?" he asked.

"Umm, I don't really know."

"Dude, I've shown you everywhere I go. There's got to be somewhere that you like going. What does Aiden like to do?"

He stuck his hands in his jean pockets and tilted his head a little. He grinned and twisted his body slowly waiting for my reply. Fuck he looked irresistible.

I thought about the reservoir but changed my mind. The place was too dirty. The park was the only place I ever frequented, at least in my childhood. But I didn't know if he'd be up for it.

"What about the park?" I shrugged.

"The park? In town?" Matte looked confused.

"Yeah, the West Texas Memorial Site. I used to go a lot when I was a kid."

"Oh. OK, let's go."

We walked around the park for a few minutes. The sun beat down on us mercilessly making me change my mind. But it was too late, we were already there.

We sat on a bench under a tree for a little while, trying to cool off. The old wooden bench had layers of paint peeling away, webs with dead insects on them, and carved initials inside a heart on one of the corners. The thought of carving *our* initials made my heart jump up and down.

As I toyed with the idea, Matte dug in my head again.

"You OK?" he asked. "You stare off a lot... something on your mind?"

I looked back at him and tried reading his expression. His eyes squinted and looked at me from head to toe. His hair blew gently with the scorching breeze. I couldn't get past how cute he was.

"Yeah... I mean no... I mean I'm fine..." I stammered.

"Why do you wear that hoodie everywhere?" He pulled at the hood draw string. "It's got to be at least 100 degrees right now."

He made a good point.

"I don't know... it makes me feel safe I guess," I shrugged.

He slid closer to me, and our legs touched again. I immediately tensed up. He put his arm on the back rest, and his masculine scent filled me.

"Take it off. Let me borrow it." He held out his other hand.

His arm glistened with sweat. Thick veins bulged and wrapped around its toned structure.

I had no response. A billion thoughts ran through my head, but I wanted to comply. I trembled reaching for the zipper. I unzipped it slowly, one tooth at a time.

I handed it to him and instantly felt vulnerable. He held it up in front of us, admiring it. He stood up, put it on, and zipped it up. The black, worn out hoodie looked better on him than it ever did on me. He put the hood on and arranged his hair inside it. I couldn't help but stare at the bulge in his jeans. I traced the pronounced head with my eyes.

"I feel safer already," he smiled. "C'mon let's keep walking."

We walked around the park, talking about bands that were coming to town and those who weren't. A lot of bands skipped West, but went to neighboring towns like Waco, Ross, Lacy Lakeview. The drive to any of those towns was no more than hour.

"Dude, did you hear The Story and Level down are coming to West?"

"No way. They always skip us. That's awesome!"

"I know! Dude, we should check on Tasting Chaos."

"Hell yeah, the line-up is pretty legit this year."

I wanted to go to all the shows. The thought that I probably wouldn't be able to pay for them didn't even cross my mind.

He pulled out his phone and typed, looked up thoughtfully, then typed again. Finally, he put the phone up to my face and showed me what he had been doing. He bought us tickets to Tasting Chaos.

"It's gonna be a blast," he said smiling.

"What! No, that's too much." My mouth dropped.

"Dude, relax. It's cool, I got it.

I couldn't believe he did that.

We ended our day at Crooks Book Store. We figured out it was the only place that we had in common. Matte had been stopping at the store at least once a week to read a book the library didn't carry, Apocalyptic Love. Who would've thought zombies and romance could make a good love story?

I had always enjoyed Crooks great selection of music. In our digital world, it was hard to find a store that still carried CD's.

"Are you sure you're allowed to come here and read their books without buying them?" I asked.

"Everybody does it, trust me."

"I-I-I don't know about this…"

As soon as we walked through the doors, he went off in search for his book. I stayed behind looking through the different covers. Cover art was one thing I liked about albums. The creativity that went into them was almost as good as the lyrics.

I picked up a CD and a kid about three years old knocked it out of my hand. He ran in circles around me for a few seconds laughing with his hands in his mouth. He stopped and looked up at me. I stared down at him, disgusted.

"Yours?" he asked pointing at the CD on the floor.

"Liam, leave the man alone. I'm so sorry sir," a young woman said. She picked the CD off the floor and handed it to me. I took it and nodded at her. She picked up the kid, who immediately started wailing, and plodded away.

After a little while, I spotted Matte in the distance. My eyes were instantly glued on him. He really did look great in my hoodie. He looked up and met my eyes. We stared at each other for a good thirty seconds. I imagined us as total strangers, falling in love at first sight.

Thousands of words, feelings, memories, and lyrics stood in the shelves between us, all part of *our* story.

He sauntered towards me, and I counted his steps. Each one was slower than the last. Time crawled. He unzipped the hoodie, took it off, and handed it to me, saying, "You ready to get out of here?"

I was ready to go anywhere with him.

I nodded and we walked out.

I struggled to put my hoodie on, missing the arm holes a couple of times before getting right. I smelled him as I zipped it up. His fresh scent filled me and made my head float away. My heart pounded in my chest, and as I walked, my steps hovered above the ground.

When we stepped outside, we stopped and stared at the setting sun. The ripples on the clouds glowed with different shades of orange and pink. The air smelled like rain and Matte, two of my favorite things. I couldn't get enough of the moment. I wanted to capture it all and keep it in my pocket forever.

I glanced over at him. He threw his head back and took a deep breath. There was something in his head again, I could feel it.

"Hey... you wanna go to my house?" he asked shyly.

He looked at my face and waited for my response.

"Yeah... let's go."

I smiled nervously. He smiled, relieved. And within minutes, we were off.

By the time we got to his house, the storm had caught up with us. What started as a sprinkle quickly turned into a downpour. We sat in his car for a second hearing the large drops of rain hitting the metal hard. It was enchanting.

"Dude, we're gonna get so fucking wet!"

"Haha, I know. It's coming down hard!"

"Fuck it dude! Haha, let's do it!"

We opened the car doors and jumped out. We kicked them closed and ran for it. Our feet splashed as we ran across the driveway. Matte stopped and jumped on a huge puddle right by the front porch, drenching us. We laughed hysterically, looking at each other as the rain poured down on us. Time felt so slow, I could nearly see each individual drop before it splashed on his perfect face.

Matte opened the front door, and we stepped right into his living room. A large L grey sectional sat before a flat screen mounted on the wall. Behind it, was an open eat-in kitchen with a glass sliding door on the wall next to it.

His parents sat at the table drinking coffee. I liked them already, they showed no shame. His mom was dressed in a white nightgown, and his dad wasn't even wearing pants. Zero fucks given.

His house was definitely at the opposite side of the spectrum from mine. One, his parents got along. Two, it was clean and well furnished. And three, it was bright and welcoming.

"Hey Mom, hey Dad, this is my buddy Aiden. We work together."

"Hi," they replied in union. I waved and smiled.

"We're gonna be in my room," he said as we walked through the living room and to the hallway.

"Move, weirdo," he said to his sister who stood in the hallway staring at us.

She wore glasses like him and rocked colorful unicorn pajamas. Her hair was long and black, pulled back into a tight ponytail. She was at least a couple years older than my brother.

"Who's this?" she asked.

"Don't bother us."

"I'm just asking, you never have friends over, only girlfriends…"

"Shut up! C'mon dude, this way."

I shrugged at the little girl and pushed through her with Matte.

We went down the hallway into his room, and he closed the door behind us. His room was the attached garage his father remodeled when his family outgrew the house's existing space.

His queen bed sat immediately to the left of the door. It was messy; pillows strewn, sheets mixed with covers, and even a T-shirt and some jeans. A dresser and two bookshelves adorned the wall to the right of the door. At the far end wall sat a single window with a large beanbag on the floor next to it.

I couldn't believe I was in Matte's room. His very own room, where he slept, walked around naked, and… who knows what else. I took a deep breath, taking in the scent of the manly room. My heart beat bruises into my chest. Things were moving so fast, my head still hadn't caught up.

"They won't bother us," he said. "Relax, let me show you around."

"OK."

"This is my bed, sooo comfortable. I don't need to make it cuz I'm just gonna sleep in it later, so what's the point? Oh, these are my favorite comic book figures. I got them when the movies released."

He grabbed a couple action figures off the dresser and showed them to me. The amount of detail on them looked expensive. He put them back on the shelf carefully and moved on.

"These are just some pics of me growing up. My mom put them up. Oh, that's Delilah, remember? The first girl I kissed?"

"Yeah, she's so pretty. Definitely not what I thought she looked like."

"I know, all the boys in my grade had a crush on her."

I stared at all the photos on the wall. There were photos of him with other girls and group photos with guys and girls. I wondered why he purposely skipped telling me about them. I guess he wanted to tell careful, calculated stories. Just like me, he was artful about what he wanted me to know.

"These are some more pics of me in high school. Freshman and sophomore, I think. Super dorky, haha."

I gawked at the high school photos. He was so young. He had braces and a couple pimples here and there. His hair was longer in both of them. I loved it. I imagined running my fingers through it and smelling it. I stared at the photos while he moved on. I wondered what was on his mind when they were taken. What did he have for breakfast that morning? Where did he go afterwards? Where had I been at the time?

"Did I lose you?" he asked.

I broke my trance and paced up to him, looking back at the photos.

"Check this out. Don't laugh, OK?"

I shrugged and shook my head.

He pulled his yearbooks from a bookshelf. He showed me his picture in each one. Sixth... short, spikey hair and a dorky plum polo. Ninth... super long hair and a "The Story" black T-shirt. Twelfth grade... long fringe with short sides and a purple plaid shirt... more like the Matte I knew now.

I enjoyed seeing him grow up in front of my eyes. The change between the years surprised me, but the name under each of his photos shocked me more than anything.

"Your name is Matte Black!?" I asked. "Like the paint?"

He laughed and said, "Yes, like the paint."

"That's fucking awesome!" I was instantly in love with his name.

"Thanks," he smiled as he put the yearbooks back on their shelves.

I imagined him in high school. I wanted to see him studying and figuring out complex math problems. I wanted to see him young and naïve making mistakes, ditching class, and eating pizza with his friends. I wanted to be one of his stupid high school friends. I wanted to see him navigate his way through life, figuring out things as they came. I wanted to be a part of the life he lived before me.

It wasn't fair that Time had kept us apart.

Against the wall lay skateboards, beat up from hours of fun in the blistering Texas sun, but sad from being forgotten. I imagined him at the skate park, sweaty and tired, frustrated

74

because he couldn't land the tricks his friends had already mastered.

They were the many faces to him that I hadn't seen. They were the faces he hid from me. I wanted them all. I wanted to relive every instance by his side. It made me uneasy not knowing who he was back then. I was jealous of those who grew up with him. I was mad at Time for not allowing us to meet sooner.

In a corner sat his bean bag. He paused for a moment, staring at it. I wondered what he was thinking. Was it special? Did he want to sit for a moment? Did... he want *us* to sit on it?

The rain came down hard. Lightning hit, and the world lit up for a second. Inside the lights flickered and snapped us back to reality.

"Sorry about that. My room is kinda shitty," he said.

He looked directly at me, scanning my eyes and my face. His hair was still damp. Droplets fell from a few strands onto his soaked shirt.

I shrugged silently. My heart raced inside my chest. My guts twisted on themselves.

"Hey, let me see your hand," he said quietly.

Without waiting he took my right hand and stared at it for a moment. He rubbed it with both his thumbs exploring every inch, every crevice as if he was looking for something. My heart pounded harder than the rain.

"You're sad..." he looked me in the eyes. "What's wrong man?"

I didn't reply. I didn't want him to know about my past. I had tried so hard to show him only what I had fabricated. But he somehow knew. He knew there was more to me than I had given him, and he wanted it.

"You don't have to tell me..." he said. "We all have our demons. Just know that I'm here for you."

I knew he knew, without having to say a word, he knew.

He raised my palm to his face and held it to his cheek. I felt his stubble and his soft, sweaty skin. He pulled me in and hugged me. My face rested on his chest, and I felt him breathe. His racing heart sent small shivers across his body. I wrapped my arms around his back and held him tight.

I was beginning to lose it. I couldn't hold my past inside any longer. I had waited so long for someone to tell me those words, to hold me like he did. My eyes watered as words and sobs crowded in my mouth. I tried to swallow but the knot was too big.

I pulled away, but he reached out. He grabbed my face with both his hands and pulled me back. Our lips met, with weeks, perhaps months, of tension behind them. We kissed softly, inhaling each other's breath as we panted.

My mind went blank. My brain was completely blank and living in the moment.

I rubbed my hands down his back before letting them rest on his ass. The male body... it's beautiful... firm, toned, different... perfect.

Our lips separated but our foreheads remained connected. We trembled in each other's arms for a moment, breathing onto one another.

He dropped down to his knees, stopping at my crotch. He undid my pants eagerly. I was heaving. I couldn't catch my breath. I held my head in my hands trying to make sense of what was happening. He buried his face into my boxers kissing and feeling what hid behind them. My dick slapped him through the fabric gently surprising us both.

He pulled my wet underwear down and stared at my penis for a couple seconds. His hot exhales tingled making it throb with excitement. Without waiting any longer, he took it in his mouth, not caring about the 105-degree day we shared, the sweat, nor the smell. He sucked me hard and deep as I grew in his mouth.

He stopped and sat me on his bed, all the while inhaling me. His stubble rubbed my balls, scratching itches I didn't know I had. I loved it. I took my hoodie and T-shirt off and threw them. The wet clothes hit the floor hard.

He moved upwards, kissing my stomach, lightly licking my tacky skin. He continued up, stopping at my heart, making a permanent residence before moving upward. He sucked my neck, engraving his name on my skin, claiming me for all eternity.

I grabbed his T-shirt and peeled it off. He undid the button of his pants as I unzipped them. I pulled them off and threw them over the bed.

I knew it. I just knew the man didn't wear underwear.

76

His thick, veiny, penis stared at me, begging for attention. I shoved it in my mouth, unsure of how to move, or what to do, or if I was even doing it right. I pulled it out and licked it top to bottom before shoving it back in. He began thrusting, holding the back of my head. I flipped him to his back and continued to suck him. He moaned and pulled my hair.

He rolled me onto my back and yanked my pants off. He put his hands on my sides and hooked my boxers with his fingers. He kissed my stomach as he pulled them off slowly.

He lay his naked body on my naked body. Our dicks rubbed together like stones igniting fire while we sealed our tongues in each other's mouths with our lips. He went down, lower and lower. He licked my asshole, making it wet with both saliva and sweat, preparing it for the taking.

I wanted him. I wanted him deep inside me. I... loved him.

He grabbed my legs and rested them on his shoulders. Sweat trickled down, and he licked it off my thighs as he stroked my dick. I wanted him.

"Fuck me," I said.

My voice sounded unfamiliar, desperate to be ravished.

I felt him rub his dick head on my asshole. I didn't twitch. I didn't pull back. I grabbed his dick and pushed the head in. I gasped and threw my arms on the bed, clenching the sheets in my fists. Time slowed to a crawl.

Matte panted and thrusted above me. His sweat rained on me, as his balls slammed my ass. My erection rubbed against our abs sending small bursts of energy through my body and strings of pre-cum to the bed. Inch by inch he satisfied me. Thrust by thrust he healed me.

The storm outside hid our passion like the secret it was.

As the rain pounded down, we both came.

Chapter 10

I stood in front of Matte's window, naked and exposed.

The storm had passed, leaving behind puddles and strewn patio furniture. I'd always admired the strength of the storms. They were so dramatic and artistic, yet violent and destructive.

I stared at the front yard. The early dawn unveiled yet another side of him that I hadn't seen.

A rusty swing set sat by the driveway. Its old and decrepit state told of the fun times. He and his siblings were already too old to play on it. Yet mom and dad refused to part ways with it.

It's hard for me to understand the attachment some parents feel for their kids. They hold on to items that remind them of their younger days. Blankets, toys, baby T-shirts, onesies. It's nothing but sentiments for forgotten times. I just don't get it.

Maybe it was that my parents didn't notice if I came and stayed or left and never returned. A hint of jealousy brewed inside me.

The swings creaked back and forth in the breeze. The old bicycles that leaned against the cinderblock wall dripped, leaving rusty circles on the hardening sand beneath them.

I drew pictures in my head in which a young Matte played with his brothers. They left their bikes and ran away from the annoying little sister who wouldn't leave them alone. She cried because all she wanted was to be part of the gang.

The hours of fun, scraped knees, and melted ice cream were the ideal pieces for children to grow into model citizens.

I imagined Matte bringing his first girlfriend to meet the family. The awkward hellos and goodbyes between them explained a defensive mother trying to keep her son young and a father proud of the catch he'd brought home.

I could see Matte getting into his mom's van on his way to prom with a different girlfriend a few years later. I imagined them dancing in a crowd of hormonal teens. I tried not to imagine their perfect night ending with them sharing their bodies with one another.

Girlfriends… it was the perfect straight life. It was the perfect straight lie.

In that sense, our lives were alike. I had many girlfriends that fueled the lie that came to me so effortlessly. To everyone I was a straight guy, a bit weird, but still hetero.

It was a lie so strong that it even fooled me. But… when had he known? When had I? I guess I kinda always knew my normal was different from everyone else's. And it had led me here, into an intimate situation with a man that was interested in me.

He had secret desires just like I did, and now we shared this sublime secret together.

He and I.

Everything happened so quickly.

I wrapped my arms around my body, holding myself together as Matte slept soundly, unaware of my state. Confusion pulled at me from all directions. His words after our encounter echoed in my head like a deafening lullaby.

"That was great," he murmured.

I looked into his eyes.

"You OK?" he asked.

I wasn't. Confusing thoughts flooded my head. I was afraid they'd spill out if I opened my mouth. I didn't want him to know. A storm of confusion or not, I had thoroughly enjoyed it.

"Matte, have you ever done this before? With another guy I mean."

He grabbed my face and stared deep into my eyes.

"No. I've been curious though. It's something I've wanted to try for a long time. I wasn't sure if you would want to. You didn't give me a lot of clues. So, I just took a chance and risked it all. But… I'm glad we got to experience it together."

"It's… I…"

I sat up. I couldn't tell him. I didn't want to ruin the moment. I didn't want to ruin the only good thing I'd ever had.

"It's OK, come here." He opened his arms and took me in.

He held me until he fell asleep, not once letting go. Our bodies pressed into each other's, silently becoming one. I was his, and he was mine.

But the guilt and confusion tore up every strand of my being. I'd love every sensation that moment gave. I couldn't sleep even when everything was perfect. Everything still remained unimaginable to me.

Where would we go from here? What would people think? Why did I like it so much? I hated myself for liking it. Sex with another guy was wrong and unnatural. It was dirty and shameful.

Snapping back to reality, I turned and looked at Matte. He was gorgeous. The soft light peeked through the shades and brushed against his body perfectly. His penis, even in its flaccid state, was desirable. His pubes, the happy trail, his abs, his ass... What did I get myself into? I had to get away. I had to think. Being in the same room as him made that impossible.

I gathered my damp clothes and got dressed. I stood before him, admiring him one last time. I stroked his leg, feeling the thin hair under my hand. I didn't want to go. He opened his eyes and looked up at me.

He reached out for my hand.

"Don't go. Stay, I want you here."

"Matte..." I shook my head.

"Please..."

I sat beside him, and he sat up. We looked at the mess of clothes and sheets on the floor before us. He placed his hand on my thigh and rubbed back and forth.

I wanted to know what he was thinking. I wanted to tell him what I was thinking. But neither of us knew where to start. Words escaped from us and hid under the evidence of our night. We looked for all the reasons we were in that room with our past and present intertwined with one another.

"This wasn't a mistake," he said. "And I know it's weird and new, but I don't care about anything. I don't want to feel guilty or sick."

80

He looked up at me, and I stared back. Everything I wanted to tell him fell to the floor and disappeared.

"Matte, I feel the same way about you. It's just... I don't know how to do this."

"Dude... I don't know either, but we can figure it out."

He reached up and held my face with one hand. He kissed me, and I kissed back without hesitation. It felt natural, almost as if we had been doing this from day one.

He slid his hand under my shirt and caressed my back, tickling as his fingers made their way down. He paused for a second above my waist and continued to kiss me. I pushed him down and traced down his ribs, feeling his tacky skin. He slid his hand down the back of my pants and outlined my crack with his index finger. The act made me gasp with both discomfort and surprise.

"Ha, sorry, we need lube," he whispered giggling.

"Yeah, good idea," I giggled back.

Matte reached for the lube in his nightstand drawer as I eagerly got undressed. I jumped back under the covers and went right for his chest. I kissed his nipples as he slid his wet fingers onto my ass. I reached for his dick and found it already wet and bulging, hard as a rock. I mounted him and slid it right in.

This had to be more than just sex right? The way he held me, the way he kissed me, the way he gently pushed himself into me, it had to be more than just a hook up.

Our silent moans blended with the morning noises in the house. His family was right outside our door starting their day. Doors opened and closed. Showers started and ended while the kitchen rattled with pans, bowls, and glasses. The dishwasher started, and the front door opened closed. One, two, and three cars started and drove off.

The whole time I expected someone to knock on our door, asking us if we were alright, or if we wanted breakfast, but no one ever did. We were alone in his room, in his bed, in our own little world.

Matte didn't cum inside me this time. Instead he came on my chest. I memorized the way he closed his eyes lightly, his messy hair, the way he bit a corner of his lips with his trembling teeth… I wanted to remember it for when I was alone, thinking about him.

He went to his desk and grabbed a towel. He handed it to me along with a kiss on the forehead. I needed a shower.

The bathroom was right outside his bedroom. I cringed at how thin the door was. Someone had to have heard something. My stomach flipped in on itself. We tried to be quiet. I thought we were quiet, but who knows? Things are different when you're in the moment. For all we know, we were as loud as a professional adult film.

Cringe.

Matte must have sensed my worry as I stared at the door. He smacked my ass as he opened his bedroom door, still naked.

"Don't worry. I can guarantee you no one heard a thing."

He was so confident on his guarantee. I guess I wasn't the first person to sleep over in his room. He spoke from experience.

Matte and I showered together. I felt a lot better knowing no one was home, and I was able to relax. I watched Matte's perfect body through the steam. He was a little taller than me, maybe three inches taller. I was only five foot seven. His flawless tanned skin wrapped around his toned structure. His arms and legs were long and slightly muscular. His ass was round with just the right amount of hair. How was it that he was so perfect?

I got a raging boner just looking at him. I reached out and rubbed his neck. I slid one hand under his arm and caressed his chest as I outlined his spine with the other. I still couldn't grasp the idea that we had fucked. We had actually full on fucked! In a way, I had taken his bisexual virginity.

"Whoa, what you got there?" Matte said grabbing my erection.

"Oh sorry, I was just…"

"Don't apologize, I just can't believe you still want more, haha."

I looked at his hand wrapped around my dick. I was much paler than him. My body was also less toned, lankier.

"It's OK, you don't have to. We should hurry."

Matte hugged me lightly, our soapy bodies barely touching. I panted. Our penis tips touched sending weakness to my knees.

"You sure?"

"Yeah... unless..." I slid a finger in his ass, and he squirmed.

"We should hurry." He smirked.

As I dried myself with a fresh towel, I looked around. Matte whistled a tune, still rinsing off. The entire bathroom had a nautical theme. Seashells lay on the sink counter and plastic seahorses hung on the walls.

I cracked open the medicine cabinet. I wanted to know him to the core. I grabbed the Aqua Reef deodorant and took a whiff. Lime and cypress, *fresh and citrusy*, it was definitely his. I applied some and put it back.

The octopus toothbrush holder held six brushes. One bathroom for six people was definitely not enough. I wondered which was Matte's; red, blue, pink, yellow, black, or purple. How could I not know his favorite color?

"Hey... what's your favorite color?"

Matte shut the water off and grabbed his towel off the wall hook.

"Purple, dude. You can borrow my toothbrush if you want."

He beamed. I gawked.

He slipped out the bathroom while I brushed my teeth.

"You can wear some of my clothes so you won't have to go home to change," Matte called out from his room.

I hung the towel on the wall hook and strolled back to the bedroom. He had laid out jeans and a shirt for me to wear.

"You can leave your clothes here. I'll wash them for you."

"No underwear?"

"Don't own any." He winked. I grinned and shook my head.

I put on his clothes taking in his scent. I loved the way he smelled. He was never the type of guy to wear cologne. He simply used deodorant and now I knew which brand.

That's how he was, simple to the max. I watched him from across the room. Today he was dressed in a blue button-down shirt and tight black slacks. The shirt fit him a little big but it still looked good. He rolled the sleeves up to his forearms and double checked the buttons were in the right buttonholes. He stared into the mirror and shrugged.

He picked up clothes and put them in the hamper. He made the bed as quickly as he could. The black sheets spread across the bed, concealing our affair, locking down the eventful night.

"I thought you didn't make the bed, what did you say? Oh yeah, 'What's the point if you're just gonna get right back in?'" I mocked him.

"Yeah, well... you know. Wouldn't want anyone to see our mess, haha."

He pulled his phone from his pocket and scrolled for a second before beginning to type. I was always mesmerized by how quickly he could move his thumbs. He wrote beautiful stories that took me to the clouds in just seconds. It was an inherent skill. No matter how hard I tried to mimic it, I couldn't.

There was something on his mind again. I wondered if something was wrong. He appeared flustered.

The phone buzzed again, and he shook his head before tapping on the screen a few more times. He went up to the calendar on the wall and then looked at his phone again. I wondered what was happening. Images of the worst possible scenarios crossed my mind.

"Is something wrong?"

He looked up at me and tapped the back of his phone with his nails nervously.

"I have a buttload of stuff to do today. I don't think I'm going to work."

He quickly dialed a number and hurried out the room. I heard him talking in the living room. His tone was different, serious, and professional. It was weird how he had more than one persona. He was a completely different person with me than he was with everyone else.

I listened carefully to piece together the situation, but noises from the bathroom and kitchen made it impossible. After a while, he came back in the room, all smiles and his hair perfectly dried and straightened.

"Mrs. Robinson's an idiot." He shook his head, grinning. "Ready to go?"

"So, you're not coming to work today?"

"Nah, I have to give my friend a ride to the doctor. Then I got a few errands to run."

84

I hated doctors. You could go in there complaining of an earache, and they'd tell you to strip to check your testicles. Perverts.

"Oh, that sucks," I said.

"I know man. I'd rather spend the day with you."

I felt my face turning red from the cheesy comment.

"Here, I made you this," he handed me a sandwich in a baggie. "Oh, and I found your phone in the bathroom."

I stuffed the phone in my pocket. He stared at it as I did. He put the sandwich in my hand and kissed me.

"Chicken salad…" he said.

"Hmm, I like chicken salad."

"I was hoping you did."

I wanted to hold his hand the entire way to the library. I gazed at it holding the gear shift. His veins bulged. Last night and this morning, that same hand held and stroked my dick. Flashes crossed my mind. His lips, his gasps, his naked body, my naked body… I still couldn't believe it had actually happened. I felt my cheeks burning up again.

I looked away and stared out the window. The world seemed different, brighter. The people on the sidewalks and in the cars around us didn't matter. They could've given us the worst homophobic looks, and I wouldn't have given one shit. I was with him, and I didn't care who knew about it.

I looked back at him. It was hard not to. The morning light made his face glow. He glanced back at me and winked. I beamed uncontrollably.

He turned into the library parking lot. He swerved left and right, trying to avoid large potholes. The seconds dug a wedge between us. It would be the first time he wouldn't be at work since the day we met. He wasn't even gone yet, and I already missed him. The agony gave me a headache. He pulled into a spot a good distance from the front door and put the car on park. I stared at my feet, searching for words inside my head.

"I'll miss you…" we both said in unison.

We laughed, and he reached over to kiss me. I figured that's why he'd parked so far from the door. In a way, I kinda didn't want Mrs. Robinson or Malinda to see us either. I just didn't know what they would think. And I didn't know why it mattered either.

I opened my eyes and saw a priest walking by the car, just a few feet from us. He stopped and stared in through the front windshield. His eyes were glued on us, trying to pry apart our attached bodies.

"Oh God, a priest? Seriously?" I cried.

Of all the people in the world, why did a fucking priest have to be the one who saw us?

"Aiden? Aiden?" Matte broke my trance. He looked back and locked eyes with the priest. "Don't pay attention to him. It means nothing."

I said nothing. The priest had stolen my voice.

"Listen, I have to go. Will you be OK?"

"Yeah... OK..."

"Have a good day, alright?"

"Yeah..."

I stepped out of the car and closed the door gently. He drove away without waiting for me to step away.

I stared at the ground and zipped past the priest to the main door. I heard him walking close behind me. His steps echoed in my ears. Why was he following me? Didn't he have people to brainwash into paying his bills or something?

The library was busier than usual. The hipsters occupied the usual areas making it impossible to get around. I had to jump over their legs to get to the breakroom. The computer lab had a line out the door that wrapped around to the non-fiction area. Malinda arranged magazines and collected money from the people that went in to use the internet. Mrs. Robinson was running around, answering questions and attempting to get people off the aisles. Mrs. Cooper helped the people at the main counter who tried to check out books.

"Mrs. Cooper?" I said out loud.

"Aiden, thank God you're here. You're late. Please, help me manage this line," she said.

"Mrs. Cooper, what are you doing here?"

"Aiden, get your badge and log in. We need to get this line down."

"It's not my day at the counter," I replied.

"I know honey, but Matte called in sick again. Get your badge and log into the computer."

"I don't have my badge. I forgot it…" *At Matte's house.*

I was still dumbfounded by her reappearance. I wasn't expecting Mrs. Cooper to come back any time soon, or at all. She had been gone almost four months. I was sure Matte would take over her position. Matte had already filled the unnoticed void.

I walked around the counter, pulled my phone out, and quickly typed a message to Matte.

"Dude, Mrs. Cooper is back…" Dot. Dot. Dot.

This wasn't good.

The first patron, a pregnant mother holding a toddler, dropped a pile of books onto the counter. Fuck my life.

A few hours into my shift, I was still lost in thought. I glanced at Mrs. Cooper expecting her to disintegrate into the recycled air of the library. But she didn't. Instead, every time I looked over at her, she would snap her fingers at me and pointed at the next person ready to check out.

People came and went as the minutes on the clock dragged behind one another. Malinda walked around flashing her smile at them. Her blonde hair brushed against her shoulders gently. Her heels clicked up and down the aisles. This was torturous.

I checked my phone to see if Matte had texted me back. He hadn't. It had been hours since I had texted, and he still hadn't replied. My stomach twisted.

"Aiden, dear God. Give me that," Mrs. Cooper said, taking my phone from my hands.

"Help Father Harry." She turned to the priest. "I'm so sorry, Father, I don't know what has gotten into this boy."

"Not to worry Mrs. Cooper. Aiden?" He cocked his head.

"Yes." I looked straight at him and scratched the back of my head.

"Nice to meet you Aiden, I'm Father Harry Lowell," he said, looking right into my eyes.

There was something odd about the way he looked at me. He had stared at me in the parking lot hours ago with the same look. Judging? Understanding? Lusting? Perhaps, who knew? I was sure of one thing, though. It was the same look Matte had given me before we met.

But Harry was a priest, a disciple of God. It wasn't possible for a man of the Lord to feel "that way" towards another man, was it?

"Is this it for you?" I asked, scanning his card and the books into his account.

"Yes, they're for a class in Sunday school. The many works of the devil," he said, grinning.

He had a few wrinkles around his piercing blue eyes, and his blond hair was beginning to grey out on the sides of his head. He was no older than thirty-six, if I had to guess.

"I don't judge," I said, handing the books to him. He stroked the bottom of my hand as he collected them.

"It's OK, I don't either," he replied with a wink.

He walked away leaving me with the weight his words and a fucking wink. What the hell?

I shook the odd event from my head and helped the next person in line.

Before I took my lunch, I asked Mrs. Cooper for my phone. After a short lecture on phone usage during work hours, she returned it to me. I sat on the couch in the breakroom and looked over my messages. Still nothing from Matte. I felt like puking. What was happening? It took seconds to reply, so why hadn't he? I tried to calm down and ate the sandwich he had made for me.

It was delicious.

After lunch, I returned to my post at the main counter. The line was shorter, and the hipsters were gone. The ambience was much calmer now. I was happy to fill in for Matte but unhappy that Mrs. Cooper had returned. I hated the old hag.

If she was back, it could only mean Matte would have to resign. My head spun with thoughts spilling out my mouth and ears. I blamed the priest. Damn him and his winking eye... the dimples that framed his smile... his perfectly styled hair.

"Agghhh get out of my head! Stupid handsome priest." I pounded the sides of my head.

At 7 p.m. I checked my phone again. Still no messages. My stomach twisted around like a strangled dragon. I bit the inside of my lips and gathered my stuff. I stepped out the front door, nearly tripping over my feet.

I sighed looking around the parking lot for his car, secretly hoping he would be waiting for me. With the minor exception from, Mrs. Cooper and Robinson's cars, the lot was empty.

I cringed at the thought of another lonely night and began my walk home.

Chapter 11

The next morning, I arrived to work a few minutes late. Everything that could go wrong, went wrong. My family left no hot water for a decent shower, so I shivered my way through a quick rinse. Cleaning crews were ridding the arroyo of trash and dead animals, so I took the long way. I hated walking the streets. People are pretty fucking terrible. But people behind the wheel are the absolute worse.

The library parking lot was buzzing as much as the streets were. Inside, the place was packed. Again. What the hell was going on? Why was everyone out and about? I stood at the entrance hall gawking at unimaginable crowd. It wasn't until a group of preteens wearing wizard capes went through the doors that it finally clicked.

School was out for summer.

Fuck.

Pastimes in West were limited. The library had the same level of *coolness* as the mall. Our usual patrons, hipsters and young mothers, were being run out of the building early by grade school kids. The little fuckers were notorious for staying around for hours, sometimes all day.

I pulled my phone out and typed a quick message to Matte: "Fuck, man, school's out!!!!"

(I purposely added extra exclamation points to show how very bad this was.)

There was no immediate response. I thought for sure that would get his attention.

I hadn't heard from him for twenty-four hours. The void in the pit of my stomach grew and my anxiety escalated. Why was this happening? Why was he ignoring me? I couldn't understand.

I slid my phone back into my pocket and went towards the breakroom. Malinda pranced by me in a hula skirt, holding hands with two little girls. One of the girls waved her free hand at me. I waved back and looked around for clues as to what was going on. The crowded children's play area hinted at one of Malinda's in costume read-along.

It was evident to me why she was the best employee Mrs. Robinson could ask for. She was always on time, took initiative, and brought innovative ideas to make the library a more family-oriented establishment. Her monthly in-costume read-along was everyone's favorite activity.

After I placed my stuff in my locker I waited in the breakroom for a few minutes, hoping Matte would walk in. The clock above the door ticked loudly in the silence. I swear sometimes the minute hand got stuck forcing me to relive the same minute again and again. Time can be so cruel.

When the door creaked open, my heart raced. Mrs. Cooper walked in. She looked terrible, older than I remembered. She had gained at least twenty pounds, her skin was blotchy, and her hair was thinning.

"Oh, good morning, Aiden," she said sipping her coffee. She coughed a couple of times. This was new. Had she picked up smoking while she was on leave? Probably.

"Mornin'." I crossed my arms. "Have you seen Matte anywhere?"

"No honey, I have not." She stared at the schedule on the refrigerator door. "Oh God, she has got to stop doing that."

I heard her talking as I walked out the breakroom. If she had no news on Matte, I had no interest in her babbling.

I checked the Men's Room and the computer lab, hoping to find him taking a leak or listening to music. Zilch. I checked the pondering area expecting to see him reading a book. Nothing. Where the hell was he?

I was heading out to the drop box when Mrs. Robinson grabbed my arm.

"Aiden, I will need you at the front desk again," she said.

"But I did it yesterday. Can't Malinda do it?"

"Aiden, what has gotten into you?

"Matte…" I mumbled quietly. Matte had gotten *into* me.

"Excuse me?" Her eyes were big and angry.

"Have you seen Matte?" I mumbled again.

"No, I have not. Now go." She pointed to the counter.

I took my place at the checkout counter and set my phone under the keyboard. The senseless chatter and laughter made my head pound. As the hours ticked away, and the people came and went, Matte remained in my head. The feeling of loss was something new to me. I had never lost anything. I mean, what's there to lose when you have nothing?

Sure, people had drifted away throughout my life. Grandpa Joel died when I was a baby. I never got to meet him. I'd heard lots of great things about him though. When I was five, I lost my best friend. Pedro's parents decided to move away. I didn't get it at the time, but I guess they didn't want to be around my dysfunctional family. In middle school, I lost my friends after I became weird and distant. But that happens. People change. People move. And people die.

I just couldn't wrap my head around losing Matte. He was special. He made me feel so… happy. He had been in my life for over two months. That's more than sixty days! We had contact every single day. We had fucked! And now… now he was just gone. I couldn't accept it.

My body felt weak and heavy. My head throbbed and spun, making my stomach queasy. I had no interest in my job or even pretending to care. People continued to bother me, desperate for help. I hated them. I wanted them to leave me alone so I could think. I needed to think!

No, I don't care about your cooking. I don't know where the cookbooks are. Shut up! I don't give a shit about your fucking party. Get the fuck out of my face. Oh your kid fell and you need a bandage? Fuck off, and take your crying brat with you, you're getting blood all over the counter. Now I'm gonna have to clean it up, thanks Karen. Oh, you want to know why the line is so long to use the computer lab, sir? Because every one of you fuckers takes forever to beat off in there! That's why!

The thoughts were driving me crazy. I needed a break. I should've fucking stayed home. Went to the reservoir. Dug a hole and threw myself into it. Anything would've been better than being surrounded by meaningless people.

"Sorry, I'm closed. I'll get someone to help you," I said to the next person in line.

I grabbed my phone from under the keyboard and made my way to the breakroom. I pressed the power button, no new messages. I needed to hear from him.

I tapped on his name and began to write.

"Dude, c'mon don't do me like this. At least tell me what's up?" I hit the send button before reading over the message. I threw myself on the couch and gripped my phone tightly. My entire body trembled as I waited desperately for a response.

My phone buzzed, shocking my body and bringing it back to life. I opened the messages and saw his name displayed with a "1" next to it. I opened his message.

"Sorry man... I've been busy. I won't be coming back to the library. Mrs. Cooper is back, and Mrs. Robinson said she doesn't have an open spot for me."

I instantly remembered the meeting with him and Mrs. Robinson. She had given him notice.

"Wait, what? So, I won't see you again?"

"We'll still see each other here and there."

"What does that mean? When?"

"Just here and there, man. I gotta go, I'll talk to you later, OK?"

Just here and there. His words echoed in my head.

And just like that, my entire world deflated. An immense emptiness crept up in my chest. My legs and arms went limp and fell lifeless at my sides. The entire space around me felt dry and dead.

I couldn't accept it. I thought about texting back or calling him. I needed to hear his voice. I wanted to hear him telling me the words that cut me so deeply in his own damn voice.

"I can't go back out there. I have to get out of here," I said out loud.

I grabbed my stuff out of my locker and made my way out the breakroom. I pushed through the crowds and out the back door of the library. The heat of the sun charred my skin as I stepped outside. Behind me, someone called my name. I wasn't sure who it was, but I didn't care enough to look back.

And I ran. I just ran.

It's funny how people create their own demises. Humans have created everything that has ever scared us. Clowns, monsters, aliens, Satan... God. My own personal favorite was drugs. When life got hard, all I had to do was drugs. Acid, molly, coke, anything.

I turned off the street and slunk into an alley. I knew exactly what I needed to feel better. My dealer wasn't too far from the library. He was the only constant in my life.

The air was thick and hot. Heat from the ground and surrounding buildings burned me as I made my way through the alley. Sweat beaded on my forehead, and my hands trembled. I imagined walking through the gates of hell wasn't much different.

"Where is he?" I asked.

He's here, just be patient.

"Where?" I asked again.

"Hey..." a man said.

He leaned against a dumpster like a dirty cowboy.

"You looking for something, bro?" he asked.

"I... I..." I said unable to complete the words.

"Say no more. Come here," he said, looking around. He flashed me toothless smile.

I stared at him puzzled as he fished inside a filthy backpack. He pulled some stuff out and knelt behind the dumpster. My eyes were glued on him, intrigued as he prepared a concoction with a spoon and a lighter.

"Hold this." He handed me the spoon. He pulled a syringe from his pocket and opened the package.

"I'll let you go first," he said. The golden fluid swirled into the syringe.

"Is this heroin?"

Opioids weren't exactly new to me, they had helped me immensely through the years, but I had never done something as strong as heroin.

"Relax brother, I don't judge. I see you looking like shit and shaking in this heat. I know what you need. I'm a doctor." He put his hand to his chest and pointed his nose up. "Now, pull your dick out."

"What?" I took a step back.

"Protection bro, just in case you croak. No one ever thinks of looking at a dick for syringe marks."

That was the stupidest shit I ever heard. But this was no time to hesitate. I needed a fix immediately. And he was a doctor, after all.

I pulled my dick out, and he grabbed it without hesitation. He squeezed it a few times, and it expanded a little. I clutched his hand. He glanced at me, then back at my dick. As soon as a vein popped up, he pricked it and pressed the contents of the syringe into me. I released my grip and exhaled deeply. My eyes went glassy, and my body melted.

"Good boy... better take a seat," he said with a leer. "It's gonna be a crazy ride."

I squatted next to the dumpster and leaned against the wall. I reached for my phone and pulled a rabbit out of my pocket. He was fluffy and white. He looked up at me and wiggled his whiskers. I petted his little body and tickled his chin. He rubbed my hand in appreciation.

The alley around me turned into paradise with a luscious stream running by my feet. The birds happily chirped in the trees, and the scent of wildflowers stuffed my nose. Fucking allergies.

"Aiden." An angelic voice cut through the scene.

I searched for the angel and spotted Harry, the priest, across the stream. He crossed it without getting wet. I admired his golden sandals and sparkling robe as he approached. His face was even more beautiful than I remembered.

"Heeeyy..." I said, handing him the bunny. "Where's... where's Jesus? Where's Jesus Fucking Christ?"

"Oh God... Aiden. What have you done?"

Chapter 12

I lay awake staring at the multitude of colors floating in through the blinds on the window. They swirled and twirled around me, painting pictures with Harry's words. I tried to find comfort in them. I tried allowing them to color over my memories of Matte and the absence of him. I wanted them to draw me a world without him, one where everything was OK and I could be happy. But nothing could do that, not even the soothing words of the handsome priest.

"Do you see Aiden?" Harry swept his hands in big circles before him. "God is amazing. He loves us just as we are; we don't have to pretend to be something we are not, we don't have to hide anything."

"Just tell me why I'm here." I struggled to sit up and put my feet on the floor.

Harry sat across from me on a chair. He wore a black button-down shirt and skinny black slacks. His hair was perfectly trimmed and parted to one side. His skin was flawless, and his blue eyes sparkled with the light that peeked through the windows.

"Oh, right. That man in the alley drugged you. God sent me to find you." Harry pointed to the ceiling and then added, "and help you." He pointed to me. "The good Lord wanted me to save you." He pressed his palms together, as if to pray, and nodded.

"He didn't drug me. I bought drugs from him and he helped me do them. Of course, heroin wasn't exactly what I wanted, but drugs are like magic erasers. They always helped me erase things." I waved my hand above my head, trying to erase the pictures that his words created.

Harry's face looked puzzled as he searched for the right words to say. He closed his eyes as if God would provide them for him.

I looked around the office, trying to familiarize myself with my surroundings. The office was bigger than the burgundy paint on the walls allowed me to see. It had large windows centered on the cinderblock wall to my left. Harry's desk sat behind him and was littered with papers and books. The wall behind the desk was decorated with large paintings of what I assumed were disciples of God. They were the same men depicted in the books my high school history teacher had, all white, all dressed in robes, all with pained faces.

I sat motionless on a beautiful brown couch adorned with purple tassel pillows. I was nothing but a stain on its perfect surface.

"How long have I been here?" I asked.

Harry broke his thoughtful trance and looked me again.

"You have been passed out for about fourteen hours, Aiden. Tell me, why did you do those drugs?"

"Listen Father, I don't want to be rude, but I need to get out of here. I appreciate you trying to help me, but I don't need help." I held my hand to my chest.

"Why Aiden? You could have died."

"Like I said, I wasn't exactly looking for heroin. I was looking for acid or maybe 'shrooms. I just took what he had. I've never done heroin before, and it hit me harder than I was ready for."

Harry bit more off than he could handle. I was a junkie just like Martia said. I relied on drugs to keep me going, to hide my past, and pave my future. I could tell Harry was never exposed to someone like me. His silence gave him away.

"You don't need that stuff, Aiden."

"You don't know me, Harry."

"I know more than you think." He cocked his head and held my phone in his hand.

I patted my pockets, "How did you get that?"

"You gave it to me when I found you in the alley. I'm sorry, I shouldn't have looked through it, but you really wanted me to find him. You wanted to find Jesus Christ. At first, I thought you

97

really meant Christ the Lord. But then you said you loved him, and you had *intercourse* with him, and now he was ignoring you."

"Give me that!"

He handed the phone over without hesitation.

I took it and turned the screen on. Matte's face displayed through the cracks, a selfie from the bathroom at his house. His face, his hair, his body, the blue shirt he wore that morning... he was perfect. That's why he had my phone that day, to surprise me with that photo. In that precise second, my heart restarted. I felt hope one more time.

"It's the same man that dropped you off at the library that day. Your boyfriend?" he asked.

My boyfriend... the words sounded so painfully perfect.

"Do you love him?"

More than you can imagine.

I remained silent looking at the photo. It encapsulated the happiest moment of my life, when everything was great, in place, exactly where it should have stayed.

"Does he love you?"

"What we have is... complicated."

"Oh." He paused and tapped his fingertips together. "I know... I know it's not easy being who you are in this time and in this town." He stood from the chair. "We are expected to follow certain customs, live certain lifestyles, and follow quiet guidelines that have been in place for centuries. Trust me, I know. It's not easy and people don't understand what we go through... inside... outside... the struggles."

I stared at him, confused. I had a feeling he no longer meant Matte and me.

"Why is it so hard for us to accept who we are?" he finished.

"I thought Jesus doesn't judge. Did you not just tell me he accepts us how we are and we don't have to hide?" I raised an eyebrow. "What exactly are *you* hiding Father?"

"It's not Jesus that we have to hide from," he said, staring right into my eyes.

He began to pace around the office looking for the words to say.

"Listen, for all we know, Jesus could have been gay himself," I said.

"What?" Harry looked disgusted and a little offended.

"I mean, think about it. He never did have a girlfriend or a wife. He had long hair and wore a dress... with sandals. He had a foot fetish, and he slept in small tents with twelve other men, who also wore dresses with sandals and never had girlfriends or wives," I said with a grin.

"Stop, just stop," he said.

I smirked and stood to leave only to find him standing directly in front me. He was a bit taller than Matte. He was so close I could feel his hard exhales on my face. He leaned down and kissed me. His lips were soft, and he was trembling. I could tell he had never done something like that, with a man or a woman. The action felt strange. Our teeth touched a couple of times. That's not supposed to happen.

But it was more than that. Something felt off. Although I'd been the object of many people's sexual desires throughout the years, I was still struggling to accept this feeling of being wanted by another man... let alone two.

I stepped back and looked at him, saw the confusion inside him. His desires fought against his beliefs and collided with his feelings. For a second, I felt sad for him. I knew the feeling. I had struggled with it for many years before Matte even came into my life. But this was something he would have to figure out himself.

I floundered to the door. I could feel him, and perhaps Jesus, too, watching me. I thought about telling him everything I had learned since Matte and I became a thing. Truth is, I didn't really know what I learned. Learning who you are and understanding who you are – these are completely different things. I knew who I was. I knew I liked men... but I couldn't understand why, and I knew I couldn't accept it. Not yet anyways.

I opened the door and lurched into the hallway.

It was obvious now where I was, the Church of Morning Glory, a massive church in the small town of West. Being a small community, West Independent School District made it mandatory we learned the history of how the town came to be. Our history teacher, being the religious nut she was, included the church in her curriculum year after year.

Morning Glory, named after the flowers, that grew in the area, unlike most Catholic churches, was beautifully crafted by skilled "men of God" giving praise to the well-funded religious organization.

The building had six offices and five teaching rooms on the left wing. The nave held enough benches, all carved out of cherry wood, for two hundred-plus people. The massively high ceilings were adorned with skylights that allowed God to hear his children. The stone walls were decorated with enormous stained-glass windows, depicting famous scenes from the Bible.

Jesus Christ is a very, very rich man.

I felt bad for leaving work without consent from my boss. And although it was Sunday afternoon, I called Mrs. Robinson. I had to keep the job, even if Matte wouldn't be there to make it bearable. I just couldn't accept that he was fired. He was an excellent employee, to my eyes, the best.

Naturally, Mrs. Robinson was furious. She screamed at me for a good five minutes before allowing me to speak. I apologized profusely and even had the nerve to ask her to consider bringing Matte back. That didn't go well. I was so stupid for even asking.

"If I bring Matte back, I'd have to let you go Aiden. I can't keep both of you."

Matte would have told her, "You just can't handle so much goodness in one small area." All I said was, "OK, I understand." I'm such a pussy.

I had the remainder of the day to myself. It was too much alone time to spend sober. The hole in my chest grew bigger with every agonizing hour. I missed Matte so much. I just couldn't accept he was out there, somewhere, without me. The world felt huge and the space between us endless.

I stared at his photo in my phone again. I memorized every detail so I could readily access it in my head at any time. God, I ached to see him.

I returned to the alley. The dealer was there again, leaning against the dumpster, waiting for his clientele. You know, in a way, he was like Jesus Christ. He helped the people of West to make it through the day, one after another. The drugs he provided where the escape from reality that we needed. Some people just can't make it through the day. We carry demons on our backs.

100

Those fuckers can get pretty heavy. We hide skeletons in our closets, some quite literal.

The dealer and I exchanged words and goods. He told me not to bring the priest again, and I promised I wouldn't. The priest was the dealer's main competitor. When people are in dire need of assistance, they turn to one of two things: religion or substance.

Combining both can make a hell of a trip.

On my way home, I decided to text Matte. I fought the strong urge to break down and tell him I needed him or I would die. So, I carefully chose my words.

"Hey," I texted.

Nothing.

"I just saw the pic you left in my phone…" I tried again.

"Nice," he texted.

Nice? That's it?

I was about to text back when another one of his came through.

"I left something in your mailbox for you. I'm sorry we couldn't spend your birthday together."

I had forgotten about my birthday. Turning twenty-two was no big deal in my eyes. But the fact that Matte had remembered instantly gave me hope. When had he done that? Probably when I was drugged out of my mind in Harry's office. I'm so stupid. I could have seen him again. He could have given me that present directly.

I ran into the arroyo. My feet wobbled under me, and the hot sun burned my neck. I put my hood on. Almost immediately sweat began to run down my face.

I made it home in just a few minutes, breathless and sweaty. I opened the mailbox and found a bag with my clean clothes and something wrapped in brown paper. There was a note taped to it, flapping in the dry air.

I opened the note and read, "Happy Birthday :)", in Matte's sloppy handwriting. I ripped the package and unrolled it. *A new hoodie.* It was black with colorful speckles on the bottom half and a thick black paint drip from the top half. I gasped and took the old hoodie off. I hurriedly put the new one on, a perfect fit. I zipped it up and hugged myself. My eyes watered as I stared at the ground.

I pulled my phone from my pocket and dropped it in the sand. I picked it up and wiped the screen on my jeans. My fingers trembled as I typed, "Thank you for the hoodie, I really like it."

"I'm glad you do."

I stood there in my front yard, wearing a brand-new hoodie, under the sweltering Texas sun. A gust flew by, sprinkling dust on my face.

"I miss you," I texted, immediately regretting it.

"I know… I'm sorry."

"I know… I'm sorry," I repeated in my head. That was all he had to say. Those penitent words and a hoodie were all I had to hold onto.

Chapter 13

Over the next several weeks, I used strips every couple hours, refusing to be sober. The sparkling galaxies collided with one another, causing black holes that swallowed everything around me. I looked at my phone more times than I needed. His words jumped out of the screen and clung to my fingers. They climbed up my arms, crawled into my ears and mercilessly pounded my brain.

Why did it have to be like this? He said so much with so little. Was he sorry I missed him? Or was he sorry he missed me too? Was I even in his head? Why couldn't he just tell me he missed me too? Why was that so hard?

Why did I keep torturing myself with these thoughts?

I went on with my empty life, silently missing "Us." Not much mattered anymore. The days at work were empty and dull. I stood on the sidelines while everything passed before me. Mrs. Robinson got a haircut and Mrs. Cooper got a scooter. Malinda went around the library decorating and chattering with patrons. Her laugh made me angry. Why couldn't she be the one who got let go? It wasn't fair that she was still here, still making my life miserable.

One day, I accidentally pushed a guy and knocked his coffee from his hand. The cup fell to the floor splashing on his trousers and shelves around him. It made a bigger mess than it should have.

"Watch it, emo faggot," he said. "Fucking hell."

I cleaned it up and put a bandage on my ego.

Later during the week, Mrs. Robinson screamed at me for not watering her plants.

"Aiden, did you forget to water my plants? Look at them, they're corpses!"

I didn't forget, I just thought they were plastic. Regardless, I bandaged my ego again.

Two nights later, my father got out of prison. He was locked up the day he got out of the hospital. I avoided prison, since my mother told the police it was self-defense. Looking at her bruises and scars, they didn't question it. The first night back, he beat her senseless.

I lay in my bed listening to the tragedy unfold. His punches echoed in the walls of the house. Furniture was thrown and dishes were broken. Footsteps pounded and doors slammed. He screamed false accusations at her. She denied, cried, and cowered like she always did. They were worse than children. Even if they don't learn their lesson, children at least try to change.

My parents had danced to the same melody for decades. Their moves were boring and tasteless. He was full of shit. That motherfucker didn't need to stick around. He could have left and continued his meaningless life without having to ruin ours.

My mother didn't have to stay with him. She carried that household on her back year after year since she was nineteen. We would have been no worse than we were with him around. Only difference was, we could've at least been able to sleep at night.

For what it's worth, Prozac did make things better. Thank you, Dexter Holland.

Time circled around me. Days blended with nights, and I was no more than a lifeless statue watching it pass. Things happened, and I allowed them to carry on. My interference had no impact on anything.

My phone turned into a brick in my pocket. It anchored me to this town and everything in it. It stopped me from floating away with the sparkles that the strips brought daily.

One day the brick vibrated in my pocket. It made my entire body tremble. It took me what felt like minutes to figure out it was my phone. I pulled it from my pocket and froze. His face displayed brilliantly behind the cracks. Matte was calling. I quickly tried to figure out it if was real or just another bad trip.

I slid my finger across the green bar and held the phone to my ear. His soft voice echoed in my ear.

"Aiden… hello… Aiden, are you there?" There he was, my sweet Jesus Christ, right at the other end of the line.

"Yeah."

"Dude, how's it going?"

I didn't reply, I couldn't.

"Aiden?" he tried again and again. I didn't reply.

"Dude, what is going on? Are you OK?"

I was pretty sure Matte didn't know I was an avid drug user. For the two months he was in my life, he was the only drug I was on. He was the best drug I ever had. I didn't need anything else.

"Dude, are you on something right now? Are you… high?" His voice was increasingly concerned.

"Yeeep."

The word felt so good coming out of my mouth. I loved the way the "p" was so strong at the end. It was the perfect ending. Why didn't more words end with that letter?

"Yep… yeeepp… yepppp," I continued.

"What the hell man. Why?" He was now agitated.

"Yep… yeeepp… yepppp," I continued. "Isn't that word awesome?"

"Dude, listen to me. You can't do that. Drugs are bad, they can kill you. I thought you were smarter than this."

"Drugs are the only things that keep me going."

"What? That doesn't make sense. You know that once the buzz is gone, your problems will still be there. It's so stupid to think like that."

In a way he was right. When I woke up every day, the first thing I felt was emptiness. I had nothing to live for, until I took something. The key was to not allow the high to fade. The key was to stay high and leave everything that troubled me behind. It's always easier to ignore your problems rather than face them, hurts way less, too.

"You don't know what you're talking about. You don't know how much this hurts. You have everything."

"Dude, c'mon. It's not like that. Listen…"

He paused. I waited and pressed the phone as hard as I could to my ear. I could hear him in the distance. His voice was muffled as if he covered the mic on the phone.

105

"Listen man, where are you? Are you home right now?"

Something inside sparked and prevented me from lying to him.

"Yes."

"Stay there, I'm coming over. OK? Stay there."

I sat on my bed with the window open. The brisk fall air chilled me. The curtains flowed with mesmerizing patterns. The walls were bare and brittle. My bedroom floor was littered with dirty clothes and lost days. The furnace blew hard, fighting the cold that I welcomed inside. I wavered between what was real and what wasn't.

Last time I saw Matte, summer had just begun. Last time I spoke to him, kids were out of school. It had been so long since he had been in my life. And now, now he was coming to save me, but how could he save me from himself?

My phone buzzed.

"Dude, I'm here. Can you open the door for me?"

"It's open." *It's always open.*

The door was always unlocked. I always left it unlocked, hoping someone would come in and finish me off.

The front door opened and closed. Footsteps moved around the house looking through every room until he stopped at my door. He opened it and peeked inside.

Our eyes met for the first time in months and just like that my insides reignited. The memory of him waiting for me in the library parking lot flashed before me. It felt so real, so warm. It was so far away.

He came in and closed the door, locking it.

"Jesus fuck, it's cold in here," he said. Without asking, he went up to the window and closed it.

"Are you OK, man?" he asked, looking at me genuinely concerned.

I glanced up at him. It felt so strange to see him in my room. He stood out from the disgusting mess my life was. He wore tight khaki slacks and a fitted black jacket. His hair was shorter, and his face was shaven. His glasses were different, too. Smaller. He was gorgeous. Perfection come alive.

"Hoodie looks good on you." He pointed at my chest.

I wore the hoodie as a daily reminder of the last time we spoke.

"Why?" I whispered.

"What?"

"Why did you leave me? Why haven't I heard from you in months?"

"Dude…"

"I have missed you so much. You have no idea how hard it has been. You don't know how much it hurts."

"Dude, I know… I'm sorry."

Why did he have to say that? Why the fuck was that the only thing he could say?

"Why can't you just tell me that you miss me too? Why is that so hard? Say it even if you don't mean it! It's not that hard!" I screamed back fighting the tears.

"Dude, I've missed you too," he said, walking up to me.

He knelt before me and placed his hand on my leg. He looked down at the floor. I knew he had something hard to say. I knew him that much. I saw him fighting against everything he hid to continue speaking.

"Aiden, it's not easy for me to say those things. That's not the way I was raised. I can't just change everything I am and how I do things."

I placed my hand on his shoulder. I didn't want to be this way. I wanted to be the easy-going boyfriend. I hated who I'd become.

"My life is complicated right now. I had to find another job, I've barely been sleeping, I've been working long hours, I'm tired… I'm sorry. You know I didn't forget about you. I've thought about you nonstop since the last time I saw you."

He took my hand from his shoulder held and held it. "I've missed you so fucking much, man."

I wanted to be mad at him. I wanted to tell him to fuck off and let me die in a drug-induced way like all the classic rock stars he admired. But… I couldn't. I loved having him in my room. I loved him too fucking much. He was my favorite drug. He made my head spun with his presence, with his scent, with his voice, with his touch.

He looked up at me. I stared back. I traced the contours of his face with my eyes, memorizing that moment and recording it forever into my mind. My heart raced. He was my existence and my very own demise. I couldn't be mad at him. It wasn't fair that I couldn't even be mad at him.

As he slowly rose, my face followed his. He unzipped his jacket, and took it off. He threw it on my dirty floor and sat next to me. Our shoulders touched. He leaned in and kissed me. His breath was clean and minty. I knew exactly where this was going. I couldn't stop it. Every bit of power I had over him dissipated, and he was in control again.

I hated that I loved every second of it. I hated how weak I was.

Matte fell asleep next to me like every cliché ass wipe in history, like *I* used to with every woman I had ever fucked. I never cared about any of them. I gave them what I thought they wanted. I fulfilled my duty like a good boy. I never gave much thought to how they felt, not once.

How did they feel after I went to sleep? Was sex really the only thing they wanted? Did they stay awake thinking about what happened, about what I felt, about what… we meant to each other? It never crossed my mind until that night.

I looked over at Matte. The soft glow of my lamp touched his face. He slept peacefully as if nothing had changed between us.

"Us," I whispered.

What were we? Friends? Boyfriends? People with completely different feelings towards each other who occasionally talked, texted, and fucked?

I couldn't understand why it hurt so much. Even having him in my house, in my bed didn't change how terrible the uncertainty felt. I rolled out of bed onto the floor and crawled to my backpack. I sat on the floor with my back to the wall, a baggie full of strips, and my eyes glued on the sleeping man in my bed.

Why was I so weak? Why did I love him so much? Why didn't he love me back?

Every concern disappeared with each strip that dissolved in my mouth.

Chapter 14

The days that followed patched up my heart little by little. I imagined tiny versions of Matte and I inside of me working around the clock, putting it together. They were happy talking, laughing, and giving each other little love gestures as they did. They held hands as they went around my body on an Easter egg hunt, finding tiny bits of my heart. Every piece they glued together made me feel worlds better.

Outside my body, *my* Matte was back. He made time to pick me up every morning and drive me to work. I ate the simple breakfast he brought me on the car ride and the sandwiches he made me for lunch.

He said I looked malnourished like I hadn't eaten in weeks. Fact is, I hadn't. I neglected my health. Not on purpose. I just didn't have the strength to take care of myself. So, Matte took it upon himself to help me any way he could. Every morning he packed an apple or a banana for breakfast along with two lunches, one for himself and one for me.

He wrote little notes and put them in my lunch bag. Most of the time they were silly jokes like, "I bet Mrs. Robinson is wearing that flowered tablecloth dress today huh?" and "You are the avocado to my toast." But sometimes he surprised me with ones that said things like, "I'll miss you" and "I like you a lot :)".

It wasn't exactly what I wanted him to say but I knew what he meant. He and I were alike in that way. It was always so hard to say something as strong as *I love you*. My parents never said it, not once. But it was hard to believe his family didn't either. They seemed closer than my family and I. They were what a real family should be.

Regardless, everything he did made me worlds happier. We spent my off days out and about. We'd lie in the park and watch the clouds float by. We'd talk about anything and everything. We'd stare into each other's eyes and fall asleep together. My stomach turned into a bubbling lava lamp every time I thought about him, every time he was with me.

Then there were the more intimate times. One night he picked me up from the library but didn't drive me to my house. Instead, he took me to his. When we arrived, I noticed the lack of cars in the driveway. I was nervous but anxious to know what was happening. When we walked through the front door, I was pleasantly surprised.

"What's this?" I asked, turning to face him with a big smile painted on my face.

"Eh, nothing much. I got off work early and decided to make you dinner."

"What about your family?"

"My Mom and Dad took my sister and brother out for dinner and a movie. My other brother moved out a little while back. It's just us for a few hours."

Matte prepared a candlelit dinner for us. I was instantly in heaven, blushing and beaming uncontrollably. I kissed him on the cheek and looked around at everything he'd done.

We ate the spaghetti and drank cherry vanilla soda while talking about work. He told me his troubles and I listened. I nodded, frowned, and smiled at the multitude of things he said. This was what couples did. We were a couple, sharing life's moments. This was... this was perfect.

As Matte put the dishes in the dishwasher, I stared at the glass doors leading to the back yard.

"What's in the back yard?" I was curious.

"Just backyardians. Wanna see?"

"Sure."

We went outside and the atmosphere changed. A cool breeze swept by, fragrant from mesquite trees nearby. That's one thing I like about the desert. It's completely different at night. It's cool and full of different smells and noises. It's a complete opposite of what days are.

We walked onto a patio. It was pitch black for a second till our eyes adjusted to the darkness, and then the sky lit up with billions of stars.

"There's almost no light pollution," he said. "Oh, check it out. You can see the big dipper and the little dipper clearly tonight."

I gawked up. How could I not notice that before?

We stared at the sparkled sky as Matte continued pointing out constellations and planets. It was so breathtaking and his knowledge kind of arousing. I simply couldn't believe I never really thought about stargazing. I'd spent my entire life in that shitty town, and never appreciated what beauty it offered. And I couldn't believe how much Matte knew about space. He was smarter than I thought.

We sat on a couple lawn chairs quietly for a moment, simply staring up when Matte broke the silence.

"Where do you see yourself in ten years?" he asked.

The question caught me off guard. The first thing that came to mind was him. I wanted to say with him, but I didn't.

"I don't know."

That felt like the wrong thing to say. I should have said with him.

"Where do you?" I tried to recover the mood. "I mean if anyone has a chance in this shitty town, it's you. Where does the great Matte Black see himself?"

He was silent briefly. Then he said, "I don't know. Rich? Famous? Or at least with the career of my dreams." He grinned at me.

"Teacher?"

"You know it… It's hard to think about that. You know? Like where was I ten years ago? Where were you?" he peered right into my eyes.

Thing is, I didn't want to remember that. I didn't want to relive those years. They were not the best years of my life. My uncle made sure of that.

"Just look at these stars. They're the same stars that looked down at us since we were born. They're the same stars that we'll look up at ten years from now and remember all of this and everything that happened before and after this. It's crazy, ain't it? It's crazy to think about all of this."

It was deep. But the only thing I wanted to remember were the times we spent together.

After we went back inside, we retreated to his room. I loved his room. His scent was engraved in every inch of it. His bed was messy and his action figures remained in the same action poses they had since the last time I had seen them. Matte kicked his shoes off and closed the door.

He lay in bed, and I rested my head on his chest. I loved hearing him breathe and feeling his voice echo deep inside his body. We listened to music, and he stroked my hair. The serenity of the moment and all those thoughts he rooted into my head, took over my emotions, and my eyes began to tear up.

"You OK? What's wrong?" Matte asked, concerned.

He sat up, and I rolled on my side, looking away.

"What's wrong, man?" Matte spooned me and put his arm around me, and then he leaned in and kissed my teary cheek.

"Fuck, man. Shit. Life fucking sucks. Twenty-two fucking years and no one has ever treated me like this. No one has ever treated me like a real person. No one but you," I said between sobs.

"Dude..."

"People haven't been nice to me my entire life, man. Not even my family. No one."

"Dude, that sucks. I'm sorry. Do you want to talk about it?"

I couldn't. I didn't. I lay in bed silently. My tears soaked into his pillow as he kissed my shoulder and the back of my head. He hugged me tighter and didn't let go. It was hard to open up and tell him my tragic story. I just couldn't tell him.

I lay wrapped in his arms for a little while, thinking about my entire life up to that point. My life was a mess. He was the only good thing I had ever had. He was perhaps the only good thing that would ever happen to me.

But I still couldn't see past the present. Everything was exactly where it should be and I still couldn't see a future that didn't revolve around my tragic past.

The first weekend in March we went to Tasting Chaos. It was easily one of the best days of my life. He picked me up at dawn. I wasn't used to being up that early. It was so early that not even birds were up yet. The crickets chirped out of view as I waddled to his car.

Matte was drinking coffee as I closed the door and clicked my seatbelt. I could tell he was having a hard time with this too. I rested my head on the headrest and fell back asleep on the way to the venue.

The drive to Waco was only a little over an hour. The tour always skipped West. I didn't blame them. Who'd want to stop at a dead-ass town? When I awoke, we were in a parking lot surrounded by hordes of sweaty people. I was drenched in sweat too. It took me a second to realize what was happening.

"Wake up dude, we're here. Here, I brought some water for you, I don't want you to get dehydrated." He yawned as I took the bottle from him.

"Thanks. How long was I out?" I rubbed my eyes.

"About an hour. But it's OK, you're gonna need all the energy you can. It's gonna be a long one. Fun, but long."

I gulped a mouthful of water and splashed some on my face. Matte walked around the car and opened my door. A gust of hot, heavy air came in the cabin. It was a thick mixture of sweat, sunscreen lotion, and hormonal youth. It's the smell of fun, a smell you never forget.

Some bands were already playing in the distance. The loud music interweaved with the roaring of crowds. Valley girls took selfies with bros who had farmer tans. A mixture of teens with their moms formed lines at booths to support their favorite bands. A couple in their thirties walked past by drinking beer from plastic cups. They were already wasted. They probably pre-gamed before getting there.

"C'mon." He extended his hand to me. I took it and we were off.

I half expected him to let go of my hand the moment we entered the crowd. He wasn't out and I sure as hell wasn't. Publicly displaying affection was risky, very risky. But surprisingly, he didn't let go. He held my hand everywhere we walked. He rubbed my fingers with his thumb and occasionally looked over at me and smiled, reassuring me that he didn't care if people saw us and neither should I.

When we stood by the stages listening to bands, he stood behind me. He held my waist and rubbed his head against mine. I felt our sweaty hair intertwine with one another. Our sweat mixed, creating a musk I can still smell today. He kissed my cheek and whispered silly things in my ear like, "I bet the lead singer has a wedgie" and "Did you see that girl over there has a mustache?"

I giggled and pressed my lips. Matte was so silly sometimes.

He continued to hold me throughout most of the performances. I felt his penis rubbing against my ass through our thin shorts. The thought of it gave me a half chub. I thought about dropping to my knees and sucking him off in the crowd. How crazy would that be? Probably not as crazy as I thought. There had to be all sorts of sexual activities going on around us. It's hard to notice those things when there's so much going on.

We walked around the different stages listening to all the different bands, some familiar and some completely new. Matte bought me a couple of T-shirts, and we stood in line to get an autograph from his favorite band. We calculated the timing perfectly as to not miss any of the bands we actually wanted to see. Before long, the fun sweaty day was over.

That evening, we drove to the reservoir and sat on the hood of his car. We watched the sun set in the horizon. The sand around us glowed, and the scattered clouds rippled in the multicolored sky. He held me in his arms and kissed me. The city fell asleep around us and after we made love under the cool night sky, so did we.

It was those sweet moments that took me by surprise. It was those moments that helped me push forward in life, even when I had no idea where I was going. He melted me every day with the heat of his love. Soon, my heart was completely recovered. Soon, I was in over my head all over again.

I wish I could tell you that everything was great, and we lived happily for the rest of our lives. I really wish it worked like that. But life is full of shit. I've been alive long enough to understand that.

One day, between text messages and happy cheesy grins, I saw Father Harry sitting in the pondering area of the library. Even

114

if I'd stayed away, he would have approached me. Because it's one of those things that have to happen. Because some of us aren't allowed to be happy.

I walked up to Harry completely unaware of the mistake I was making. He looked up at me, flashed a smile and motioned me to sit with him.

"Hi Aiden. How have you been?" He asked.

"I've actually been really good, thank you. How about yourself?"

"I've been great. You know, just doing the Lord's work."

I smirked and rolled my eyes at the remark. How can anyone be so naïve as to believe in something as insipid as God?

"You know, Matte and I have started seeing each other again," I said.

I was ready to tell him everything about us. I knew that out of everyone, he would understand. He was the only one knew about Matte and me.

Then maybe someday I would tell my mother and brother, then my grandma, and maybe even Mrs. Robinson and Malinda. I wanted my whole world to know about Matte and how I felt about him.

"Yes, well actually that's why I'm here today. I was hoping to talk to you about *Matte*." He took off his reading glasses and put them in his shirt pocket.

The way he said Matte's name was the biggest clue I missed.

"Oh yeah? What about Matte?"

"Let me backtrack a little bit. You may have caught wind of something last time we spoke." He looked at his hands as he fidgeted. "Throughout the years, I have accepted *how* I am. But as you know, it's different accepting yourself and being accepted by others. It hasn't always been easy and following in Gods footsteps makes it harder."

He paused and examined my expression.

"The first time I saw you two was the very first time I saw two men… kissing. It made me feel something inside, something I didn't think I wanted. But I was curious. Then I didn't see you and him together. I was worried at first. Then I went on a mission to south Texas and upon my return, I saw him dropping you off here.

115

You seem so natural together, so happy, so full of life. It's like he completes you."

I felt my face burning. I felt foolish... foolishly in love.

"But I don't think you complete him..." He shook his head and squinted his eyes almost as if he expected me to explode in anger.

My heart fell and anxiety brewed inside me. "What do you mean?"

"Now, calm down. I may be wrong about it, but it seems like he might have ulterior motives to this relationship."

"What does that mean? What are you trying to say?" I demanded.

"I just don't think he's good for you, Aiden, that's all. I think you can do better than him. I think you can find someone who will be what you wish Matte was."

"Someone better?" I asked, mocking him. "Someone, like who? Like you?"

"I am a good person. You know that." He held a hand to his chest.

How dare he? He didn't know Matte. He didn't know me. He had never fucked anyone. For fuck's sake, he had probably never even been in a relationship.

"You don't know me." I stood and turned my back to him.

"Aiden, please listen to me."

I looked over at him, and he stared back.

"Fuck you. What would you even know? You've never even kissed anyone, how can you sit there and think you can give me relationship advice?"

"I've kissed you..." he winked.

"Ha, you forced yourself on me. That's what all you 'men of God' do. You force yourself on people. You prey on the weak. Suck my balls bitch," I said, grabbing my crotch.

I took my phone out of my pocket.

"So, what's up?" I texted Matte.

"Nothing much, just thinking about you," he immediately responded.

"Me too, I can't wait to see you."

I was too worked up to let myself be swooned.

"Wanna come over tonight?" he asked.

116

What kind of question was that? Of course I did.

"For sure," I replied. "Pick me up?"

"Can't, I'll be busy till eight. Meet me at my place?"

"Ok, I'll be there."

The rest of the day dragged ass. I couldn't focus on my duties enough to get Harry out of my head. His words bounced back and forth within the walls of my skull, bruising my brain. What did he mean Matte wasn't good for me? Matte was the best thing that ever happened to me. No one had ever cared about me as much as he did. But the biggest question, the one that made my stomach turn, was... why? Why did he say those precise words?

At 7 p.m. I walked out the back door of the library, just like in the old days. I couldn't bear running into someone who could take any of Matte's time. Someone like Malinda. She would've cornered me and talked a bunch of bullshit like she always did.

And, to be honest, I was also a little afraid of running into Harry. Who would've known being afraid of a man of God was a real thing? I guess I was just afraid of asking the right questions only to get the wrong answers.

On my walk home, I decided to text my mother and ask to borrow her car.

"Mother, could I borrow your car? I really need it."

This was one of the worst times not to have a license. Half the time I asked, she declined. If she did this time, it would take me forever to get to Matte's. Thankfully, this wasn't one of them.

"Sure," she texted.

Matte lived about twenty minutes from my house give or take. I drove ten miles under the speed limit, just as my uncle taught me. The handful of times I had been behind the wheel were all on his lap and all at least twelve years ago. I remembered everything he taught me, how could you not when you don't even want the lessons?

But, driving ten miles under the speed limit was torturous. I hit every red light and got stuck behind every slow driver in fucking West. Why did this shit happen every time I was in a hurry?

I remembered the drive to Matte's perfectly from the times he drove us there. It was by the truck stop, right at the

McDonald's, past the arroyo, and another right at the empty lot with the tall sand dunes. Matte's house was the fifth on the left next to the only tree on the block.

When I pulled up I noticed a strange car parked in Matte's driveway. A friend of one of his brothers? A neighbor's? Perhaps a relative? I dismissed those ideas.

I parked by the tree and decided to wait a few minutes to see if anybody came out. I bit my nails and tapped my feet. After I chewed my nails, I bit the inside of my lips. I only stopped after tasting my own blood. I waited five minutes, and no one came out. Whoever was inside the house was there to see Matte. But who? And why wasn't I aware of this?

I shut the engine off and stepped out. The warm March air added to my regret. *I should've stayed home.* The walk to the front door pulled me down. My arms were cold and distant from my body, and I dragged my stomach behind me. I don't know why I allowed anxiety to tear me apart before I knew all the details. But deep inside, I knew my gut was right this time.

I rang the doorbell and listened carefully for signs of life, a struggle, a conversation, anything. I heard a door open and close and some muffled speaking. The front door opened, and Matte's face lit up. Fuck he looked fine as hell. He wore a tight navy T-shirt and washed out jeans. The bulge was on point.

"Hey," I said.

"Hey man. C'mon in."

I stepped into the living room, my heart ready to jump out of my chest. Everything looked the same, sofa... loveseat... recliner... all covered with throw pillows and a couple blankets. Everything was exactly the same, but it didn't smell the same. It smelled different... like expensive body lotion. It wasn't irrational. Matte did have a mother and a sister. But would they wear something expensive like that?

"Let's go to my room," he said smiling.

I smiled back.

Matte lead us to his room. My eyes were glued on his figure. Rock music flowed out of his room, scremo. I knew Matte didn't like that scremo shit. He was more into classic rock. He pushed the door open and we stepped in.

118

I saw her standing by Matte's bed, looking through his tablet. She was a few inches shorter than us, pale flawless skin, impeccable style, perfect smile, deep green eyes, and bright red hair. She'd probably curled it before coming over. She wore red heels, fishnet stockings, a black dress, dark lipstick, and eye makeup. She was punk rock perfection.

She glared at us as we walked around the bed to her. She put the music down and smiled, never looking away from my eyes. My heart was pounding, fucking hell was it pounding.

"Clarissa, this is my buddy Aiden... Aiden, this is Clarissa, my girlfriend..."

Chapter 15

Who knows why we do the things we do when we're in love?

We allow our foolish feelings to dictate what we are and aren't allowed to do. And those emotions, the attraction, the ridiculous idea we are meant to be... blinds us. We continuously lie to ourselves. We tell ourselves everything is OK. We demolish ourselves to the point that as long as the other person is happy, that's all that matters.

We are so caught up in the fear of losing that special someone that it's difficult to accept that sometimes we might be in love with the wrong person.

I should've left the second the words rolled out of his mouth.

I should've walked out the door and never looked back.

But I didn't. I couldn't.

I swallowed the pain and forced out a smile.

"Nice to meet you, Clarissa," I said.

She took a couple steps towards me, straightening her dress and fluffing her hair, never taking her eyes off me. She hugged me tightly, almost as to let me know where I stood in this fucked-up food chain.

She smelled like him, like his Aqua Reef deodorant, like his sweat, like his kisses... like my boyfriend. My head flooded with clear, crystal sharp images of them together messing around, fucking just before I rang the doorbell. I imagined her pissing his jizz out and wiping her cunt, satisfied and accomplished. He didn't have a chance to wash his dick before he came to open the door. If I went down on him right then, I could probably taste her.

My body stood dead, hollow, and loveless. My empty stomach filled with anger, jealousy, and sadness.

I glanced over at Matte. He gazed at her with my eyes, with the same eyes he once stared at me. She grabbed his hand and rubbed the outside with her thumb. He moved in closer and grabbed her waist. She turned around and clung to his neck as he held on to her.

The make-believe world that I had created shattered and fell upon me, suffocating my insides and starving them of the life I fed them. I couldn't understand how I had been so stupid to allow yet another person to gain possession of my life. The man I loved stood five feet from me, holding someone else.

They laughed, caught in each other's eyes with the passion and desire of sweet, tender love. They occasionally broke trance and looked over at me. They spat words that pounded my eardrums with giant mallets. They were intoxicated with one another's presence and their mannerisms slapped my eyeballs, desperately trying to make me understand that I shouldn't be there.

I wanted to run from the pain. I wanted to escape the prison my mind was creating. But I couldn't. I wrote my sentence and accepted my fate.

"So how long have you two been together?" I tried to join their conversation.

"We've dated on and off for two years." She waved her hand in front of her face as if she tried to fan off the smell of her breath.

Two years?

Matte and I had been together off and on for ten of those months.

"Wow… two years… that's a really long time," I said.

"Yeah, it's been a weird, rough two years but here we are." She rubbed her fingernails up and down Matte's back. "How long have you two been friends?"

"We met in May last year, a few days after my birthday actually," Matte interrupted, releasing his grip on her waist.

I refused to look at him. I knew I wouldn't be able to hold it together. I would start crying the second I did. Instead I kept looking at her. I nodded my head as I scoped her head to toe. I could see why he liked her.

I felt inferior. Seeing them together, so well put together, I was no match. They were perfect as individuals and even better as a couple. I knew I wouldn't stand a chance in the battle for him. They had history, a rocky, shaky, long history.

What did we have?

A million thoughts crossed my head, all of them screaming at me to leave. I refused. I needed to stay. I needed to keep torturing myself.

Free will can be pretty fucked up sometimes.

"Aiden?" Matte said.

I finally looked up at him. I wish I hadn't.

"You with us, buddy? Clarissa just asked you something."

"Oh no, it's OK. I was just being silly."

"No, I'm really sorry. What was it?" I rubbed the back of my head down to my neck.

"I was just saying you look like a nice guy, and Matte is a real asshole sometimes. I'm surprised you are friends with him. I asked why?"

Matte wasn't an asshole. He was perfection at its finest.

"Oh yeah, well, you know how that goes," I said.

She looked away and played with her hair. I looked at my feet and twiddled my fingers. Matte looked at both of us and scratched his head. Whatever his plan had been, it had failed. How could it not? Having both of us in the same room was the worst thing he could have done.

"Um... you guys wanna go somewhere?" Matte pressed his palms together, probably praying for this to be over.

"Yeah, let's go for pizza, and then we can go to the mall or something. Matte said you were single, right?" Clarissa pointed at me.

There it was again, another jab to my heart. The pain was too real.

I shrugged.

"Well, maybe we can find a cute girl for you to talk to or something."

I remained silent, fiddling with my hands.

How much longer could this charade continue? How long till I snapped? Or Matte snapped? Or even Clarissa? It was like trying to put two magnets together on the same magnetic pole.

"Ookay, let's go before this gets weirder." Matte clapped his hands together.

"Oh, let's take my truck. It's bigger and we can ride more comfortably," Clarissa cupped her chest.

Truck? Who was she trying to kid? That thing was not a truck. It wasn't even an SUV. It was merely a crossover, a weird blend between a car and a minivan.

I walked towards the front door, leaving them behind but listening closely. I didn't want to miss anything. I tried to be aloof. But in reality, I was a fool.

The second we settled into Clarissa's car, the plans changed for the worse. Matte decided we should go to the bookstore instead of the mall. He wanted to finally buy the book he had been reading for months.

I didn't want to go to Crook's. That was our place. Why? How could he do that to me?

"Are you sure you want to go to Crook's? It's sooo boring, that place is for nerds."

"Babe, you know I like books."

"But books are so old. Who reads books anymore? Audio books are the thing now, if that's your thing."

"Maybe, but you just can't beat the feeling of holding someone's own writing. Plus, Aiden likes books, too. I'm sure we can find a nerdy girl for him there. Right, bud? What do you think?"

I saw Matte looking at me through the rearview mirror, waiting for me to chime in.

"In a way I agree with Clarissa. Physical books are kinda outdated. Audio books are the present."

"See?"

"But I agree more with Matte, there's no greater feeling than holding something that was written by talented people. They're more than pages filled with words. They're words pulled directly from someone's head. When holding a book, we're holding their thoughts and ideas. We're holding months, years of hard work. The feeling is almost magical."

"You see, Aiden gets it."

Clarissa poked her finger in her mouth, insinuating we made her want to puke.

The ride was uncomfortable at best. Clarissa was a total nutjob behind the wheel. She swerved between lanes on the highway and honked at an old man for driving slow in the slow lane. Matte fidgeted with the radio trying to find a good station. Clarissa had satellite radio, the possibilities were nearly endless.

I sat quietly in the backseat. I stared out the window wondering how this could be happening. Matte and I had been parading around town as a couple. How had we never crossed paths with her?

As we walked through the doors, I excused myself to use the restroom. I walked through the history shelves of the store, thinking and shaking my head.

"Fuck, what the hell is going on? This can't be happening. What's his plan? Why is he doing this?" I murmured to myself.

Would I get a second to speak to him without her? I could text him, but what if she saw? That could make more of a mess.

I burst into the men's room and stood in front of the mirror. I saw the sadness melting my eyes. I opened the hot water and stuck my hands under the faucet. Within seconds, the water stung my skin like a billion needles. The pain distracted me from the reality of the situation. I didn't know what to do or if anything could be done.

After a few minutes, Matte stormed in. He walked past me to the urinal, then back. He stood inches behind me. I felt his body pressed lightly against mine. I looked up at him on the mirror. He grabbed my arms and turned me around to face him. He stuck his tongue inside my mouth. He kissed me long and hard. I felt our growing erections meet and greet each other.

I pulled back and pushed him away. I didn't know what was happening. I didn't know how to react, how to continue. I looked at his face. His eyes were watery, and his lips pressed together. He was a familiar stranger. He was Matte, but he wasn't *my* Matte.

My head was pounding, and I was hot. The thought of us behind Clarissa's back made me sick to my stomach. It's not easy being a secret, especially when you don't want to be one.

Everything that went through my head, everything that I wanted to tell him rushed to my mouth and bottlenecked at my throat. I didn't know the words that would make him understand that I wasn't onboard with what he was doing.

"Dude… what the fuck?" was all I could say.

He remained silent for a minute then said, "Aiden, c'mon man. Be cool."

"Why?" I asked. "Why like this?"

I didn't know what my words meant. It was as if I spoke in a different language, one that I had never spoken before. They were the desperate words of a beaten man.

"Dude, I thought you'd be happy. I thought you would like to have me in secrecy. You know, like we're each other's secret."

"How can you expect me to be happy? You think I'm happy to feel this way? You think it makes me happy that you refer to me as your 'buddy' Aiden?"

Matte shook his head slowly. He traced my entire face with his watery eyes and sighed.

"Do you think it makes me happy to see you holding her hand? Kissing her? The way you look at her, the way she looks at you? Why would you think that would make me happy?"

He stared into my eyes and searched for words that didn't exist.

"I need you. I want you and only you. Why would you think I want you and your girlfriend of two years? Two fucking years, Matte? How? Why?"

"That came out wrong." He pointed at me. "I just want you to be safe and happy. I thought you would be OK if you were around."

"Around? Around you and her?" I pointed in her direction out the door.

"I thought you would be better with us than out doing drugs. Drugs are bad for you, man. Can't you see that?" He grabbed my hand and held it against his chest.

"No dude, you are bad for me," I said both lightly pushing him and pulling back my hand.

His eyes shot to the floor and he stood silent for a couple seconds.

"I… I guess I'm no better than drugs, huh?"

The truth does hurt. He turned away and began to walk towards the door.

"I'm sorry…" I said.

There it was again, me trying to protect whatever that fucked up broken thing was. It was pathetic.

I reached for his arm. He didn't try to pull away, and I didn't try to pull him back. It was a missed opportunity. It was a moment of making it or breaking it, letting him go, or keeping whatever I could.

"You're all that I've got. I don't want to lose you." I looked at him with tears in my eyes, with my last breath.

"I don't want to lose you either. I'm gonna break up with her, I just need to figure out the right time and place. Trust me…" He took my hand and kissed it before walking out of the restroom.

I did trust him and for longer than I should have, I believed him.

We ended up leaving right after the incident in the restroom. Matte told Clarissa I was sick to my stomach. He said he wasn't feeling too hot either. He apologized, and she believed him. We sat in silence on our way back. The radio played classic rock, barely audible. Matte and Clarissa didn't speak. They didn't hold hands or look at each other, and when we got back to his house they didn't hug or kiss goodbye. It was weird and awkward.

Matte went inside, I got in my car and drove off with Clarissa close behind me. At the light by the truck stop, I went right, and she went left.

When I got home, I found my father's truck in the driveway blasting music. I parked my mother's car next to it and listened for a few minutes. I could always tell what went through his mind according to the songs he played. He listened to the tracks that took him back in time. They were the same country songs he listened to throughout my childhood.

The music took me back in time with him. I thought about everything bad that had happened throughout the years up to that second.

I shut the car off and stepped out. I peeked in the cabin of his truck to find it empty. I opened the door and turned the music down. Through the dim light, I saw beer cans on the cabin floor

126

and the neck of a bottle peeking from under the seat. I knew why he did it. I knew why he drank himself stupid. He drank to return to the past, and he drank for the future. I wasn't much different than him. I hated my past and feared my future. We had different poison, but the same exact reasons.

"The hell you do that for?" he said, appearing from the shadows.

I glanced at him, head to toe.

"Answer me you piece of shit!"

I remained silent.

"Where you been all night?"

"Out."

"*Out*," he mimicked me. "You fucking queer."

I stared at him in disgust. His eyes were yellowed, hair was thinning, and his face was wrinkly.

"Get out of my face, faggot," he said, spraying my face with spit.

The years hadn't been good to either of us.

I walked up the driveway to the front door only to find it cracked open. Inside the house, I saw the signs of a struggle: a broken chair and a trash can full of glass shards. I closed the door behind me, and his music started blasting again.

The house was dark and quiet, the hallway dimly lit with the glowing phone screens within the bedrooms. My mother lay in bed, probably wishing it'd be different. This couldn't be the life she saw for herself as a child. She was trapped in this windowless, doorless box with the only two things of value she had in her life. My brother lay sprawled out on his bedroom floor, watching videos of other people's lives. It was a life that he'd never have a chance to live. To him, it was all make-believe.

The screens went off as I made my way to my room. I couldn't help them.

I took my clothes off and crawled under the covers. I thought about Matte. I replayed our conversation in my head. Why was this happening? Why couldn't I have just one thing? Just this one thing? Why was that so much to ask for? I needed him. I wanted him to talk to me, to apologize, to assure me that everything would work out.

"Hey," I texted.

"Hey," he replied.

I couldn't bring myself to force a conversation. Instead, I looked at his picture, wondering if I was anywhere in his head, and fell asleep.

At dawn, I frantically looked for my phone. I found it wedged between the wall and the mattress, dead. I plugged it in and waited for any signs of life. Zero percent came up on the screen, relieving my anxiety. I left it on my nightstand charging while I got ready for work. I went about my routines and a few minutes later, we were both on our way out the door.

Matte had texted me while I slept. The time read 2:43 a.m. and his words filled me with hope.

"I will break up with Clarissa in the morning. We're supposed to meet before work."

I didn't like the idea of them hanging out, but it had to be done... I suppose.

When I got to the library, I spotted Harry chatting with Mrs. Robinson by the front counter. I had the urge to avoid him but at the same time, I kinda wanted to talk to him. Something inside me wanted to know everything he knew.

"Good morning Aiden," he said with a big smile as I walked past.

"Hi, what's up?" I called back.

He ran up to me as I made my way to the employee breakroom. He talked so much, so fast. It was hard to keep up.

"Aiden, the other day... those things I said, I said them because of something I saw."

"Oh yeah?"

I figured as much. In a way, I was happy he'd instigated. He helped me push forward the inevitable.

"Well, I saw them together again today," he continued waiting for any reaction. "Matte and a girl, I saw them at a bagel shop having breakfast."

"I know. They had something private to discuss."

I didn't want him to know that Matte had been seeing us both for some time.

"Aiden, I might be overstepping my boundaries here, but I don't think she's just a friend."

I felt my walls closing in, slowly suffocating my already ruined lungs.

"What did you see?" I whispered.

He sighed.

"They held hands. They kissed. They left together in the same car, his car. They looked very much like a couple."

I envisioned them together having breakfast. I imagined them going back to his house and finishing what they started the day before. She felt his sweet lips while running her hands all over his body. She knew every inch of it just as much as I did, maybe even better. They would lay in each other's arms intoxicated with passion and desire, and I would be pushed away to the deepest corners of their minds.

To her, I was her boyfriend's creepy friend. To him, I was his darkest secret.

"So, what do you think?" Harry asked.

I looked over at him, confused by his question.

"I'm sorry, what?"

"Would you like to have lunch with me today?"

The thoughts of Matte out there with her came to a stop. I looked at Harry's soft blue eyes, and I was tangled. He was welcoming me into his life without knowing how much of a fuckup I was. But even if he did know, he would patch me up because that's what he did. He did it as a pastor, and as a genuinely great person.

"Yeah, I'd like that," I said, giving him a thumbs up. "Pick me up at one."

His face lit up, and he flashed me a smile. With that one look, he promised to help me forget what I needed to remember.

"Hey, by the way, I'm sorry for what I said the other day."

He shook his head and waved his hand around like he was trying to shoo away a fly.

"Don't worry about it, Aiden. It's water under the bridge."

The hours crawled by. Images of Matte and Clarissa painted the walls. I threw strips in my mouth on the hour, every hour. But there weren't enough drugs to help calm the pathetic pain I felt. It was pain that I brought upon myself, wounds that I inflicted on my being simply by hanging on to something forced.

I don't know why I allowed my own fears to dictate what I did. It was just easier to fall back into drugs than to deal with everything head on. My brain created such clear pictures of what they were doing that I simply had to accept it. It was true. It had to be. Everything I thought they were doing, they were probably doing to some extent.

My drugs eased me into a life that was hard, and now they helped me with the idea that I was no longer who I thought I was. The thought that Harry could be a shoulder to lean on popped into my head. He was there, letting me know of something that I would otherwise be oblivious to. That was more than Matte was at the moment.

By lunch time, I was out of my mind. I lay on the carpet in the children's play area surrounded by stuffed animals and mega blocks, so much like my everyday life. I was surrounded by fake people inflated by their selfish ways living in a fake world built on their lies.

Harry stood by my side, disrupting my self-induced fantasy, breaking me free from everything that incarcerated me.

"You alright there Aiden?" he asked.

He stretched his arm to me. I grabbed his hand. It was soft and clammy.

I immediately began to wonder about his body. Was he hairy or smooth? Did he work out? He seemed fit, too fit for a pastor. I wanted to run my fingers under his shirt and feel him. I wanted my hands to wander down his pants and feel his soft cock. I was now sweating.

"Oh Harry, you're so silly," I said as he lifted me up.

He put his arm around me and, I placed my hand on his chest for support. I felt our hearts racing. I looked at his face, his eyes, his lips, and the thick vein on his neck that carried blood to his penis. Oh boy, I really wanted him.

"Are you okay, Aiden?" Mrs. Robinson asked catching us off guard.

"Yes, uh, we were just..." I spluttered.

I retracted my hand from Harry's chest and waved around like a wand.

"We were just heading out to lunch Mrs. Robinson, no need to worry," Harry reassured her.

"Oh… OK. Well, uh, hurry back. I need you to watch the computer room this afternoon, Aiden. Malinda has a doctor's appointment and will be leaving early. Father Lowell, I will see you later."

"I'll see you in church on Sunday, Mrs. Robinson."

"Oh dear, yes, of course."

Chapter 16

We sat in a patio across from each other, our hands mere inches away. Street noises blended with nature creating a perfect atmosphere of natural and man-made. Birds chirped in the canopies above us, leaves rustled in the trees, and cars drove by. The heat expelled from their engines mixed with the heat from the sun and brushed my skin with painful strokes. It was surreal, and my high made them almost magical.

One thing I learned about Harry right away was that he loved talking. His mouth moved so fast, and his hands were all over the place. They talked almost as much as his mouth did. He reminded me of an anime character. Not a main character, you know? He was more like the supporting character that you ultimately end up loving more than the main character just because of how cute and weird he is.

Harry was an open book, keeping nothing a secret. I sat there listening and staring at him, propping my head up on my fist like a boy in love. I don't know if it was that I was high or that I hadn't eaten all day, but Harry was truly a handsome man. There was something enchanting about him, something virginal that pulled me in. He was the epitome of a saint. He was a fucking hot saint.

I stared at his long fingers holding the spoon that dropped sugar into his coffee, one dazzling crystal at a time. He mixed it in slowly, the spoon clinking against the porcelain cup. The action hypnotized me, and I was all his.

Father Harry Lowell had been with the ministry of the church for over fourteen years. Morning Glory was like a second home for him. He had attended the University of Texas Arlington and studied philosophy with a major in theology. He became an ordained minister at the age of twenty-six, finally fulfilling his boyhood dream. He was so much older than me. But it seemed he had his shit right even when he was younger than me.

"After I graduated college, I came back to West. I just love it here, you know? Life is so much slower in these small towns, although it hasn't always been a walk in the park. But, I love the weather. So, here I am. Oh, and my mom lives here, of course. I can't even imagine my life without her. I love her, she's such a sweet lady. She's the strongest woman I've ever met. She's always been there for me. She's the only one who ever believed in my dreams. She's my number one."

Harry flashed a grin. He talked about his mom almost as if she were a lover. Ew.

"No brothers or sisters?" I asked.

"No, my dad left when I was just a tiny peanut. My mom never remarried. It was just her and me."

"That sucks."

"No, it's OK. I forgave him. God had other plans for him."

Growing up as an only child wasn't easy for Harry. Of course, not having a father didn't help either. A strong independent woman should be sufficient when raising a good kid like him. But sometimes, there are a lot of things that go unnoticed. Even when you think you've got it, you really don't.

"What did you mean 'it hasn't always been a walk in the park?' Seems to me like you all did pretty alright."

I toyed with sugar that had spilled on the table, making little lines. Harry held his hands together, interlocking his fingers. He stared at my finger as I played with the sugar, and sighed.

"Kids are just awful." His eyes shot up at me. "They say the darndest things, you know? My mom just wanted me to be a good kid. She didn't want me to be a hoodlum."

Harry told me about his childhood. He drilled deeply into everything that broke him year after year since grade school. Girls teased him for the way he dressed. They made fun of the clothes his mom picked out for him.

"Aiden, they laughed. They laughed hysterically at my face like I was some sort of clown act. I told them, 'Collared shirt and slacks are the appropriate attire for success,' but they just laughed like I told them a joke."

I shrugged.

My heart ached for Harry. I wanted to jump back in time and bop those little bitches on the head. But that was ludicrous. Time travel was impossible, and I didn't even have words to help him. The little girls would probably talk shit about me too. I imagined them saying, "Nice shoes. Where'd you get 'em? Walmart?"

I am no hero.

"Sometimes they would walk up to me, that girl Tiffany and her friends. They would ask me stupid questions like, 'You don't have a dad? How does that happen? Mommies need a daddy to have a baby.' You know my mom, bless her soul, she never told me girls and boys were different. I always thought we were the same. I even envied them for wearing dresses and having long hair sometimes. After a while, a rumor was going around that I was a test tube baby."

A single mother, no father, and no siblings create the perfect ammunition for young kids who have it *all*. Harry's childhood was almost as twisted as mine.

Boys are usually a little more brutal when it comes to bullying. They often have older brothers, cousins, or *uncles* who tease and wrestle with them. They teach them how to defend themselves physically and verbally. They also teach them the more obscure things of life.

Harry didn't have that.

"Then in middle school, someone started this rumor that my mom was a 'fat lesbo.' They said my mother and I were gay together. They chanted, 'Harry has the gay cooties. Harry has the gay cooties.' I mean that's not even possible. If my mom was a lesbo and I was a queer, we wouldn't be sleeping together, not a chance Jose."

The boys at school teased Harry for changing in the stall during gym class. They accused him of doing so to hide his boner from seeing all of them in their underpants. Some of the boys even went as far as pulling his shorts down in front of the other boys and humping him over his underwear.

"My mom was furious, Aiden, you should've seen her. Like a bat out of hell. She marched down to the principal's office and demanded the boys be expelled. You know what the gym teacher said? 'It's simple dominance behavior. All boys do it.'"

He crossed his arms and pushed out his chest mimicking the teachers' mannerisms. I tried imagining Harry and his mom at the principal's office. I couldn't. Harry seemed so mature and grown up, it was hard to picture him as a child.

"And the principal backed him up by telling her, 'This is perfectly normal. It teaches them where they stand in the food chain.' I mean the audacity of these men!"

The 90's were fucked up times.

I didn't think Harry was a loser. I think he was simply misunderstood. Like me, he had shifty direction in life. Yes, his parents divorced when he was only two years old, and he didn't have siblings. But also, his mother had a terrifying fear of him growing up to be a hooligan. So, to protect him, she never allowed him to hang out with other kids outside of school. The few kids with whom he had a connection simply moved on and made friends with normal kids. At home he had no internet access and TV was limited to PBS and televangelists programming.

I mean you can only learn so much from Caillou and Mr. Copeland. Those two men are fucked up. No one should be exposed to that type of shit!

"The only man in my life was Jesus. He was always there. He told me everything would be alright."

"You actually spoke to Jesus?" I raised an eyebrow.

"Yes, Aiden. Keep up. Jesus came to me in a dream. We walked together in heaven. He told me what to do. He told me to hang on."

His eyes were so wide.

Harry loved church and believed Jesus was his only real friend. His mother would often find him talking to him in his bedroom. He said she wasn't able to see him because she wasn't a true believer. His mother "believed it," and soon, she too, could speak to Jesus. In a way, the invisible zombie became both a husband and a father in that household.

Imaginary, yes, but better than the father I had.

"Jesus told me to go to church. He said, 'You will be good friends with the ministers. They will show you the way to heaven.' So, I did. As I grew older, I spent more and more time at Morning Glory. I spent all my free time there. And you know what? By the time I was in high school, I was good friends with the ministers at the church. Jesus was right! They understood me and accepted me as I was, without judgment. For the first time in my life, I felt like I fit in perfectly."

He paused to take a sip of coffee.

"They never... you know?" I asked.

"Never what?"

I didn't want to say the words, but I was curious.

"They never... touched you?"

Harry almost choked on his coffee. He grabbed a napkin and coughed into it.

"Touched me? Ew, no."

I was relieved they hadn't, kinda. For a second, I thought maybe they had, then maybe I could have talked to him about it. That was selfish, I know. I'm sorry.

"What about you, Aiden? Gosh, I feel like I've been rambling on and on. Tell me a little about yourself."

I couldn't tell him much. In contrast to him, I was a demon. I was a homo junkie, embarrassed of the pathetic life I had. How could I tell him about watching R rated movies since birth, drugs, sex, and abuse? It ain't easy. There are no soft words to describe hard stuff. So, I crafted a shell of a life that was easy to digest.

"Oh, where to begin. Umm, I have a mother and a father. They're OK. They haven't been around too much. I have a little brother. He's only seven. He could be my own kid. I think he was kind of a mistake, like me, I guess. My grandma lives in West, too. I like her, she's nice."

Perfect. Short and sweet.

"Gosh, that's beautiful. I love older people. They've seen so much, lived through so many things. You know?"

I nodded.

"But you're not a mistake, Aiden. You're perfect just the way God created you."

I shrugged, neither agreeing nor disagreeing.

"Oh, have you ever had butter pecan ice cream? It's the absolute best. I had it down south when I was on a mission. They have it here at the mom and pop shop down the street. C'mon, let's go get some. You'll love it."

I continued to see Harry, quite often. I started stopping by the church every morning. The less time I spent at my house, the better I felt. Harry was at the church early daily. He'd have a fresh pot of coffee and doughnuts in his office. It was the perfect breakfast. I'd stick around for an hour, listening to his stories and eating doughnuts until he left for his morning meeting. We said our goodbyes and then I'd be on my way to the library.

He was just one of those people that are easy to talk to. I didn't even have to say much, he did all the talking. And when I did have something to say, he was there ready to listen. I guess that's why I kept coming back. He was always there. I needed that, especially since Matte started to fade into the background once again.

Time with Harry was very different than time with anyone I'd ever spent time with. Less tense. Very relaxed and effortless. My face lit up when I saw him walking in the library, and I loved that he waited for me in the parking lot after work. It was very reminiscent of the years I spent with Martia. Unlike her though, he talked about Jesus and his chores. He told me about activities planned for the weekends ahead and how enthused he was.

"Aiden, you should really come by the church bazaar in a couple weeks. There'll be tons of activities and food."

"I don't know. I might burst into flames surrounded by all the churchy people." I wiggled my fingers at him like magic wands.

"Naw, don't be silly. C'mon, it'll be fun."

"Maybe."

He huffed and shook his head.

"OK, that's all I need right now. A maybe."

He slapped me a high five. A freaking high five! What was up with people and high fives?

Harry's words always made me feel better. He was the sweetest person, male or female, I ever allowed into my life. But as sweet as he was, I felt like I wanted more than just someone to talk to. I found myself constantly pushing for something else. It wasn't his charisma that attracted me, well, not entirely anyway.

I wasn't sure how to make him aware that I wanted *him*. I wasn't sure if he would even be up for it. He had kissed me… and he had asked me to 'hang out.' I was sure after a few weeks we were friends, but I felt we had a chance for something else.

So, I pushed for more every chance I got. Whenever I handed him something or took something from him, I always made sure to rub his hand. I grabbed his arm when we said goodbye and when we said hello. I stood by him closer than I needed to so our bodies would touch "on accident." It felt like a game, but he seemed to like it. He grinned every time I did something risqué. It was a weird something-ship.

The most memorable time was when he accidently touched my penis. My constant erections and wanking sessions wouldn't let me forget that one. That day we were unloading his truck from goods he had picked up at the Ross farmers market. He went on and on about the great selections and awesome deals they had that day.

He always walked faster than me, but I didn't mind. Harry had a delicious looking ass. It was toned and round. Each cheek was like a loaf of freshly baked bread. I wanted to eat it along with the meaty sausage he packed in front. The slacks he wore daily left little to the imagination. And boy did I have a big imagination.

We walked together down the hall that led to the parking lot. With no warning whatsoever, he slowed down. He rambled on and on while I counted the tiles on the floor when suddenly, out of nowhere, his arm went a little too far, and he grazed the tip of my penis through my shorts.

"Oh God, I'm so sorry, Aiden. I didn't mean to." He jumped back and held his hands to his chest, dropping the bags of goods to the floor.

"What?"

"I didn't mean to touch your penis. I'm so sorry."

My penis was already at a half chub and clearly visible through the fabric. Harry had barely touched it.

"Relax man, I think he liked it." I wagged my hips back and forth. My penis swayed happily with the motion.

138

Harry stood there, staring at my crotch. His face turned as red as the tomatoes he'd bought that morning. It was the cutest thing.

We always had a lot of fun. He made me smile and laugh every time I saw him. He was so adorable and innocent. I couldn't get enough of him.

But it wasn't all sweet nothings during those times. Although Matte was distant, he was always lurking just around the corner. It had been nearly a month since he promised to break up with Clarissa. He hadn't yet. He'd text me about hanging out with her occasionally. His words left little to the imagination. They made my eyes bleed tears of pain.

He told me about the time she jerked him off in public. She kissed him and slid her hand down his pants while at the movies. They went home, and he fucked her in her bedroom with the door wide open. Her family watched TV in the living room, completely oblivious to their indecencies.

He told me about eating her out in the stairwell at her college between classes. They were almost caught by a security guard making his rounds.

A few days later he fucked her raw in the janitor's closet. He texted me a picture of the cum stains on his shirt where he wiped his dick because he had nothing else to wipe it on. He followed the picture with one of his dick as a consolation price.

I cowered in my seat every time.

I often wondered if Clarissa knew about us. I wondered if she saw him texting me after their passionate affairs or sneaking off to the bathroom to text me dick pics during commercial breaks while watching TV. But if she did, then she was as big a fool as I was. We were both players in Matte's twisted game.

And the more I allowed him to hang out with her and fuck her, the more Matte accepted me as an object in his life. I was no longer his boyfriend nor his lover. I wasn't even sure if I was still his friend.

Through him, I knew her. I knew details about her life that most would consider secret. I knew what her favorite sexual position was, how big her areolas were, her "haircut" downstairs, her favorite food and drink, her grades, previous boyfriends, siblings, I even knew what birth control she used.

It was almost as if Matte wanted me to see her as he did. But I couldn't. How could I when she was replacing me? Each time they were together pushed me deeper and deeper into a hole I could not escape. The more I clawed at the walls of my entrapment, the bigger the hole grew.

The more I clung onto Matte, the more this fucked-up game killed me.

Chapter 17

Within weeks of hanging out, I already knew Harry as much as I knew Matte. I also knew I was starting to *really* like him. After the hurricane I'd lived through with Matte, my life came to a complete halt with Harry. He was a ray of sunshine, always happy, spreading through the darkness of my life. He attracted me in ways that Matte never did. And I found the more we hung out, the more I wanted to fuck him.

He, of course, had other ideas. Sometimes he welcomed my advances, and sometimes he'd squirm and start rambling about Jesus. He'd jump away and would tell me random facts about the good Lord. He'd walk around, going off, ranting about how he wished he'd been alive at the same time as Jesus was.

I get it. The man turned water into wine. It doesn't get much cooler than that. But at some point it's like, c'mon man... give it a rest.

I wasn't sure what I was doing. And I wasn't entirely sure if he saw me the way I saw him. In my experience, sex always came before any sort of relationship. As much as I tried to compare him to Matte, I couldn't. Matte handcrafted our relationship. Things with him had evolved naturally. All I had to do was be open to the idea of being *loved*. Matte was perfect.

Harry was worlds different. Everything was new to him: from the innocent "accidental" hand touching to the time he bumped my penis. And through all the accidents and purposed touches, I'll never forget our first time.

It happened that spring when I helped him set up the annual bazaar that led up to Easter Sunday. It was something completely out of my comfort zone. I never liked being in public surrounded by strangers, let alone at a church. Harry had been asking me to come to church for several weeks. The closer the bazaar got, the more relentless he became about it. I declined multiple times before he convinced me in the weirdest way.

"So, you're coming to the bazaar this weekend, right?"

I sighed.

"I don't know, man. Those things aren't for people like me."

"Please Aiden, pleeease. Pretty pretty please."

I fiddled with my fingers silently.

"I just really wanna waste time with you," he said.

I stared at his face, speechless. It was the exact phrase that Matte used on me. It had to mean something.

"What did you just say?"

"I wanna waste time with you?" he squinted his eyes as if I was about to punch him.

I jumped at the idea immediately.

"Ok, let's waste each other's time," I replied smiling. Harry was ecstatic.

He picked me up early that morning. Immediately, I was surprised at how different he looked. He wore tight jeans and a loose-fitting long sleeve button up, untucked. A baseball cap and sunglasses completed the ensemble. I almost didn't recognize him.

"Hi Aiden, how are you today?"

"Harry… you look different." I looked him up and down. My eyes shot to his bulge. I had never seen Harry look so… tasty.

"Oh yeah, I didn't want to ruin my good clothes. Plus, it's gonna be a hot one out there. You ready?"

I shook my head still stunned by his look.

"I guess."

"Alright, let's go."

As soon as we got to the church, he sent me to stand with the other helpers. Many of the workers were fellow Catholics, but some looked like punks doing community service for a misdemeanor. At a different time, maybe I could have scored some drugs from them.

142

We gathered around in a large group. Some people drank coffee while others drank energy drinks. A guy spit on the ground and stepped on it. He looked over as I stared. I looked away instantly.

Harry assigned tasks, and people dispersed.

Some people went off to the kitchen. There was a lot of cooking to take place. I glanced at the food items for sale on a flyer some kid was handing out. Pulled pork sandwiches, nachos, hot dogs, and hamburgers were on the menu. It was a lot of cheap and easy stuff to make.

I didn't know if I should help put up tents or head to the kitchen to help. It shouldn't have been a hard decision, but it kinda was. Did I want to be out in the sun? Or did I want to be in an air conditioned building? I chose the latter.

Helping in the kitchen wasn't as easy as I thought it would be. I tried to make myself helpful as much as I could but for the most part I was in everyone's way. I didn't know what a "cheese grater" was when a lady asked me to get it. I looked everywhere in the kitchen for a notebook titled "cheese grader." I'm so stupid, why would anyone want to grade cheese?

After the mess in the kitchen, I decided to go outside and try harder work. Harry and I didn't work together for the most part. That was kind of a bummer. But he was always around. Any time I looked towards him, I caught him looking at me. He smiled and waved every single time. I gave him a shy wave and looked away grinning.

I lost sight of him around noon. He went off to the bouncy houses, leaving me completely surrounded by strangers. Little gangs of kids ran past me, nearly tripping me. A few minutes later, a group of older kids came through running, looking for the brats. I pointed them in the direction they went, and they left.

A girl, easily thirteen, stayed behind. She twisted her hair in her fingers and tried making conversation with me.

"So, what's your name?"

"Aiden."

"Cool. I'm Carly. You don't go to church huh?"

I shook my head.

"My parents make me. I hate them." She tried sounding cool. As if hating parents was something I would find "hot."

"What do you do for fun? Do you go to parties?"

She bit her thumb while scoping me top to bottom.

"Carly! Carly!" Someone from the group of older kids called out for her.

"I gotta go, bye!"

It was the weirdest thing. I shook my head and tried to make my way through the crowds before someone else singled me out.

"Hey, boy, you in the hoodie," some man with a baby on a backpack called out. He looked tired, like he hadn't slept in days. I only realized he was talking to me when I noticed I was the only one in eighty-degree weather wearing a hooded sweatshirt.

"Yeah?" I replied.

"Could you do me a huge favor?"

"Uh, sure."

"Please go in the church, into my office. It's the one next to Harry's, you can't miss it. I've seen you here before."

"OK."

"There's a stack of notebooks and boxes of pens sitting by my desk, could you bring 'em to me? It was a donation that I forgot to bring out to sell." He handed me his keys and I took them.

The baby strapped to his back reached his saliva-soaked fingers out to me. His eyes were crusty, like he'd been crying, and his nose was runny. I could tell it had been a rough few days for him and his dad. I shook my head at him and pressed a smile. No way in hell would I let him touch me with his gross-ass hands.

I strolled towards the building, swinging the keys on my finger. The church itself was closed as the bazaar took place on the grounds. The main doors were obviously visible from the tents. So, I decided to take a side door. I figured if people saw me going in, they'd want to come in. People are funny like that. They like expanding. The more space they see, the more they want to occupy.

I tried the door, and it was locked.

"Seems legit," I said out loud. My voice startled me in the silence.

I went through all the keys until I found one that worked. I unlocked the door, went through, and locked it behind me. I took a left at the lobby and made my way down the long hallway that held the offices, bobbing my head to the music outside. I'd been there with Harry so many times, I had the place memorized. Although a bit dark, the hallway felt serene. The paintings of Bible depictions weren't even that creepy.

I sauntered down the hallway, admiring the work. When I reached the man's office, I shuffled the keys around looking for the one that would unlock the door. That's when I heard a noise coming from Harry's office. Instantly, curiosity got the best of me. I put the keys in my pocket and went to investigate.

I opened the door expecting to see a strange face, but to my surprise, found Harry. He looked up and waved. I smiled and gave him a small wave.

"Hey, whatcha doing here?" he asked.

"Oh, uh, your buddy with the baby backpack asked me to get some stuff from his office. You?"

"I needed to get away for a second. It's just too much fun out there, I can't even," he replied.

I couldn't tell if he was being sarcastic or for real. He did love being involved in everything. But, I guess at some point too much is too much.

He sat on the corner of his desk and rested his hands on the flat surface. He stared at me and sighed as I awkwardly stood by the door. He cocked his head to the side and swayed his feet back and forth. He looked absolutely charming.

I left the door cracked open and walked up to him. His eyes glanced at my feet and slowly made their way up. We stared into each other's eyes, figuring out that we were alone. Something that we weren't expecting of today was about to happen.

"Man, it's so nice what you do out there. I can tell those people really appreciate everything you do. You're truly a different type of person compared to what I'm used to."

I meant it. No one in my life was as nice and genuine of a person as Harry was.

"Thanks, I try. It's just so doggone hard sometimes." He fisted one hand and scratched his neck with the other.

I sat on his desk next to him, closer than I intended. Our fingers accidently touched, but neither of us moved away. I looked at him, and he stared back at me. His cheeky grin made me smile and look away in embarrassment.

"Whaaat?" he said swaying his feet faster.

"Nothing. You're just so cute," I replied grinning bigger than ever.

The roar of the crowd outside filled our quiet space like a perfect song to mark the moment. Time slowed, and our breathing got heavier through our cheesy smiles.

There was only one thing in my mind, and I wondered if it was the same thing in his. I moved my hand to rest on his. His warmth felt delicious against my cold fingertips. I looked back at him. We gazed at each other and traced each other's lips with our eyes.

He leaned in, and I leaned in. Our lips met, trembling. I grabbed his face and pressed it against mine, kissing him harder. No teeth this time. I wondered if he'd been practicing. He smelled like a perfect blend of sweat and cologne, a concoction created from hours in the sun.

We panted. I wanted more. I could tell he wanted more.

I jumped off the desk and kissed his neck. I undid the buttons on his shirt, slowly. His hands caressed my back and came to a stop above my hips. He left them there, motionless for a few minutes, collecting my sweat. He was a master of restraint. Anyone else would already have my dick in their mouth.

I pulled his shirt off and dropped it on the floor. He squeezed my ass and kissed my neck. I traced my hands down his back then onto his lap, then finally his crotch. I rubbed his dick through his pants, making him gasp quietly. That made me harder. I brushed it in circular motions. He let out a loud moan and immediately covered his mouth.

"Don't come yet, Harry," I whispered.

I unzipped his pants and lay him on his desk, knocking over papers and pens. His eyes shot to the open door then back at me, insinuating I should close it.

"Nah," I said. Part of me wanted to give the saints in the hallway a show.

I pulled his pants down, exposing an erection under white briefs. I buried my face in his crotch and took a deep breath. I grabbed on to the waistband and pulled them off in a hurry. His

146

penis was wet. His penis was actually wet with anticipation. And I gotta say, I didn't picture Harry as someone who'd completely shaved his lower regions.

I stared at his perfect body, sculpted by God himself. I took his penis in my mouth, and he covered his eyes with his palms. I traced up and down the shaft then down to his balls. He gasped as I munched on his ass. He moaned and called out for Jesus. I never thought he'd use the name of the Lord in vain, but there he was loudly whispering, "Oh Jesus oh oh Jeeesuus."

I spit in his ass and fingered it gently, getting it ready. Matte taught me that. Harry rubbed his nipples in tight circles. I spit in his ass again and pressed the head of my dick onto his tight hole. I pressed on slowly, inch by inch, until I was balls deep. He held his head with his hands and bit his lip.

I had longed for that moment since our first lunch together. I had jerked off so many times to images of his bodacious bulge and tight ass. I had wanted to pound that ass for so fucking long. I'd cum to the feeling of his hand accidently touching my dick time and time again.

This was the last bump in our weird something-ship, and now we'd just jumped over it. Everything would have to be easier after this. Or at least I thought.

I pulled out all the way then went back in. It was easier the second time. I thrusted and thrusted, smacking his ass with my balls each time. I fucked him raw and hard until he came all over his smooth abs. I rubbed my hand over his cum and pulled out. I jerked off with his jizz and came all over his dick. Globs dripped from his balls to the tiled floor.

His office was no longer the only truly innocent room in the church.

That night, I sat against the wall outside my bedroom window. I stared at the darkness that extended past my backyard and into the cotton fields behind the house. I couldn't stop thinking about Harry. Flashes of our intimate moment crossed my mind, giving me a raging boner. Air escaped my lungs in long sighs. I still couldn't believe it. I had taken the man's virginity, in the house of God. We had committed the ultimate sin. I had singlehandedly secured his place in hell, and it was next to mine.

I grinned at the image of Harry and me in hell, holding hands and eating ice cream. Brimstone and fire, the devil's own recipe. Fuck, Jesus would be so upset at him.

This wasn't over. I wanted more.

The next morning I woke up to a text from Harry. It was a bit unusual since he was more of a caller instead of a texter. It's kinda funny how much different a generation can be.

"I can't stop thinking about you :)" he texted.

The time stamp on it was 5 a.m. Oh, Harry, you early bird.

"Me either," I texted back.

"You should come to church this morning," he texted back instantly.

"Harry, I came at church yesterday. We both did."

"Very funny, Aiden."

I loved teasing the man. It was so easy.

Since Harry was at church, and Matte was M.I.A., I decided to take a walk. Being alone in my room with my thoughts wasn't a good idea. The nightmares continuously threatened to come back.

I got dressed and used the restroom. I listened carefully for any signs of life in the house. My father snored loudly in the living room. I knew no one else would be up. It wasn't in their best interest to wake him.

I went to the kitchen and took some crackers. I put them in a baggie and threw it in my backpack along with a bottle of water. I tiptoed past the living room to the front door. My father lay stomach down on the couch. Empty beer cans and pork rind bags surrounded his slumber. He was a pathetic piece of shit.

I walked out the door and closed it lightly behind me.

There was no plan. I was just going to walk around town to tire myself out so I could go home and sleep. Then I'd get up the next morning and go to work. That was it. That's all I had.

Everybody always talks about having a purpose. Purpose this and purpose that. What was my purpose? Nobody ever tells you what purpose you have. You're supposed to figure it out yourself. But when? How? I was twenty-two, and I still hadn't figured shit out. When would my time come?

I plodded across the field that led to the reservoir, kicking the sprouts that pushed their way out the dirt. I found it interesting that even cotton plants looked young when they were. Within weeks they'd grow to full-blown plants. The plants then developed pale yellow flowers that'd turn pink when mature. The flower then dried and created a bulb which then grew until it cracked open revealing white fluffiness. It was just like people, from baby greens to white-headed boomers.

The resemblance was kinda funny to me.

Then there were the few that never made it to maturity. Weeds took over the plants that weren't cared for properly. They impaired them, making it nearly impossible to create the crop. I was one of those few. I was wasted space.

When I got to the reservoir, I jumped into the arroyo. It was the quickest and easiest way to get to the library, which was at the far end of town. I walked a couple of miles before noticing I was being followed. When I heard the whimpers, I immediately thought a coyote would jump out of the brush to attack me. I turned around to find a small dog some ten feet behind.

I gazed at it for a few seconds. It looked at me and lowered its head. Its tail was shyly tucked between its hind legs. I took a step towards it, and it backed up, afraid. I felt sorry for it. Its ribs were showing, and it had patches of hair missing. I wanted to help but didn't know if I could. Then it hit me, I could at least give it some food.

I took the crackers I had packed in my backpack and held the bag before me. I shook it, and the dogs ears perked up, indicating it had an owner at some point. I looked around for something to lay the crackers on and found a large rock. I walked towards it and emptied the bag onto it. I looked at the dog and whistled at it.

"Come here, baby, have some food."

It stared at me, unsure if I could be trusted.

"C'mon, it's all yours." I kneeled before the rock.

The dog wagged its tail but refused to get close to me. I knew I'd have to leave before the dog went to eat.

"That's OK, I wouldn't trust me either."

I stood and turned to walk away. I continued my stroll, looking over my shoulder every few steps. The dog approached the rock and ate up the crackers. It looked over at me and wagged its tail. I was happy to think I helped the little fella out.

Harry offered to pick me up from the library Monday night. Anything was better than going home, so I agreed. I was even hoping to spend the night, but I didn't want to be pushy.

"So, what do you wanna do, Aiden?" he asked as I got in his truck.

I put my face up to the air vents to cool it. The air was cold and refreshing.

"Umm, get some food maybe?"

"Nice, me too. What do you feel like eating?"

"Your ass?" I grinned.

Harry let out a nervous giggle.

"Just kidding, man. I'm OK with anything." I said sitting back on the seat and clicking the seatbelt on.

"Wanna come to my house? I made some stuffed shells last night, my mom's recipe."

"That sounds good."

And we were off. Harry didn't live far from the library. It was honestly just a few streets over from my house. But as close as it was, it felt worlds apart. His neighborhood was clean and kept up. Not a single house in the block had piled trash by the curb, or junk cars in the driveways.

Harry's house was a small three-bedroom brown brick ranch. The front yard had a flawless lawn with a white picket fence adorning it. Two small flower beds lay on each side of the red front door. As we walked inside, I noticed the sprouts on one of the beds looked like watermelon plants. I'd have to come back once the fruit grew.

The inside of Harry's house was as pristine as the outside. It smelled like fresh linen, and the open layout gave a full view of the kitchen, dining, living, and bedrooms. The walls were eggshell white and had framed photos of him and a strong chinned woman with short, spiky hair.

"Is this your mom?"

"Yes, isn't she the sweetest woman you've ever seen?

"Umm, yes?" His mom did look like a fat lesbo.

Harry smiled and took his shoes off.

150

I took my shoes off too, mimicking my host. The floors appeared to be hardwood. Harry was a 'hardwood' type of guy. The furniture, from the living room set to the dining room, all looked unused. Or barely used at best. He was really a well-kept guy.

"Make yourself at home. I'll warm up the food."

I didn't know what "make yourself at home" meant. At my house, all I did was hide in the emptiness of my bedroom. Whenever I was alone, I felt the darkness of my thoughts creeping in.

Oh no.

"Umm, it's OK. Maybe I'll help you out."

"Aw, OK. You wanna grab some plates from that cabinet?"

I helped Harry get the plates. He loaded them up with the stuffed shells and poured extra sauce on them. He microwaved them as I poured us each a glass of water. We sat across from each other and had dinner. I gazed at him and smiled. He cocked his head, beamed, and gave me double thumbs up. I nodded and gave him a thumbs up back. The action made me feel weird. I wasn't the thumbs up type of guy.

The food was delicious. It was a legit home-cooked meal. I couldn't even remember the last time I had enjoyed one. This was really nice.

"Would you like some wine to go with our meal?" Harry got up and walked to a cabinet by the kitchen. He came back a few seconds later holding up an amber bottle and a couple wine glasses.

As surprising as it seems, I didn't drink alcohol that often. The most I had ever drank was beer with Martia, and that was ages ago.

"Sure."

He poured us some wine and set the bottle down. I don't know why I was so nervous to drink in front of Harry. He had seen me drugged out of my mind before. A little alcohol shouldn't have been a big deal. But it was. I didn't want to ruin what we had worked so hard on.

"Oh, my God, this goes really well with the shells, try it."

I stared at the red liquid in the glass. It had a rich cabernet color. I took a sip and gulped it down. I hated the taste but it warmed me up instantly. I took another bite of food and followed with another sip of wine. What do you know, they did go well with each other.

I'm not sure why, but I thought Harry would like to hear about the dog I saw over the weekend. The wine probably had something to do with it. The alcohol loosened me up, and I felt the strong urge to speak. I waited until Harry took a drink of wine so I wouldn't interrupt his story.

"Dude, I saw a dog in the arroyo the other day."

"Oh yeah? You think it was a stray?"

"Yeah, I think so. He seemed kinda hungry, so I gave him some cheese crackers I had in my backpack."

"Aw, Aiden! That is so sweet." He put his hands up to his chest. "I bet you made Jesus smile."

I stared down at my plate blushing. I played with my food for a few seconds, thinking about Harry's perfect words. Everything he ever said was perfect. With him I never had to second guess what I said. I never felt embarrassed or stupid. He accepted me, flawed or not. I wasn't used to the feeling.

After dinner we strolled around his neighborhood, talking and laughing. The air was warm with a hint of coolness rising from the ground. His neighbors watered their lawns as kids rode around in their bikes. The birds chirped away noisily in the surrounding trees and squirrels ran from one another across the front yards.

Everybody waved hello as we passed by. I was surprised at how well-known Harry was. I was in the presence of a small-town celebrity and didn't even know it. It made sense though. He was the nicest person I ever met. He was kind to me and everyone else we encountered.

I felt safe. With Harry, I always felt safe. But Matte made me feel alive. I didn't know what was better, safety or pain.

At the end of the block, we turned around to make our way back to his house. We paused for a few minutes in front of someone's yard. Harry talked loudly to one of the neighbors. I stared at them as they chatted about the weather. My eyes drifted to a speck of blue a few feet from us. I walked towards it, entranced. It was a blue condom. It was partially sundried and partially filled with fluid. I towered over it for a few seconds before Harry came to a halt beside me.

"Ew, get away from that Aiden. I can't believe someone would just throw that on the street."

Thoughts of a possible perpetrator flooded my head. Someone's dick had been inside it, thrusting wildly before filling it up with warm, gooey jizz.

"Aiden, let's keep walking. I'll let the neighborhood watch know about it."

I looked at Harry, then back at the condom. His words fought against my thoughts. I was a stronger person now. Somehow, I knew I didn't need the perverse acts. Somehow, I was able to walk away leaving the past behind.

We sat on the bed of his truck in the backyard watching the sun set in the horizon. The breeze was warm and inviting. Birds chirped loudly, getting ready for bed. The rustling of the leaves on the trees around us played the perfect tune for the serene moment.

We stared into the distance in silence. I wondered what went through his mind. There was nothing on mine. I didn't have to go anywhere. I didn't have to pretend to be someone or wish to be someone else. I was with him, watching the world pass us by. And it was perfect. I was living in the moment, alone with him.

Chapter 18

Harry and I continued to hang out that spring. Even though we had been intimate, every time we fooled around felt like the first time. His body never felt familiar. He acted like I had never licked his neck or ate his ass. He gasped and startled every time I touched him.

But sometimes, he'd bring up a new kink. It was as though he had watched a video of someone doing something and he wanted to try it. He started out innocently, by touching my belly button. Apparently, he'd never seen an outie before. He liked licking it and toying with it. Before I knew it, he was having me eat cheese puffs out of his innie.

Maybe he was just trying to figure out what he liked. Or maybe he wanted to try something he thought *I* would like. But it felt as if he was the divine fruit I wasn't supposed to eat. We fooled around and made out a few times, but we hadn't fucked again. It had been weeks since our office sexcapade.

Hadn't he enjoyed it as much as I had? Had I? Or had I just tricked myself into believing that I had as a way to forget Matte? Maybe it was the fact that I couldn't forget Matte that prevented us from moving forward. I hated that he was in my head even when I had already decided to leave him behind.

I loved that Harry stopped by the library on his way home almost daily. Every time I saw him walking in, I'd get that nervous anxious feeling in my stomach. I'd hear his nasally voice and it'd send me on a frenzy. I'd come up to him with open arms and would want to hug him. And as much as I did, I didn't. Because what we had was complicated. It was sweet, innocent, and secret.

I loved that he stopped by every day so much that on the days he didn't, I'd stop by his place on my way to my house. I wanted to be around him nonstop and I knew he did too. In a way we had become virtually inseparable.

But I found that whenever he wasn't around, Matte would infiltrate my mind. I'd lay on the roof of my house at night, and he crept in. I'd be walking to work, and his shadow walked behind me. Even though I rarely ever heard from him anymore, he was always there. He always lingered in the back of my mind, reminding me that we were still "pending."

Matte became like an annoying song stuck in my head. The more I gave in and replayed it, the more loudly it played. The louder it played, the more it interrupted my daily activities. And soon, I started thinking about him and Clarissa even when Harry was around.

It choked me to think that he was somewhere out there with Clarissa. It killed me to think that she'd spend the night with him, that she'd kiss his dewy skin during their crazy nights, and that they'd wake up together in his bed wrapped together in his sheets. And when they whispered in each other's ears, all time would stop.

I knew it too well. I missed it too much.

One day, Mrs. Robinson sent me home after lunch. Apparently, Malinda had told her that I looked sickly. Of course, she had walked in that morning when I was puking my guts out in the breakroom. I knew she'd rat me out the second our eyes met.

I lay on the couch trying to regain control of myself when Mrs. Robinson walked in. She hovered over me for a few seconds before saying, "Aiden, honey, you don't look well. Malinda told me she saw you throwing up. Please, head home before you get worse or get someone else sick."

I was too weak to put up a fight. I couldn't eat, and I couldn't sleep. There was simply no time for it in my days. I spent so much time thinking and processing things in my head. It had taken over my entire life. I gave Mrs. Robinson a nod, collected my things, and marched out the back door.

I strolled by the park, hiked by the reservoir, and then went home. It didn't matter where I went. I heard them in my head at every stop I made, at every turn I took. I saw them everywhere. It was bullshit. How could he drop me like that? It was inhumane. Why wasn't I even worth a second of his time?

I couldn't take it anymore, so I decided to contact him. I pulled out my phone and stared for a moment. What could I possibly say?

"Hey," I finally texted.

I waited for a reply, wondering if it would ever come. I stared at the phone again. It was the only remaining link we had. Our relationship or friendship, or whatever it was, had become nonexistent.

The phone came to life with Harry's name. It buzzed away in my hand.

Fucking Harry.

I answered the call and allowed him to distract me.

"Hi Aiden. Whatcha up to? I stopped by the library and Mrs. Robinson told me you left early."

I was silent, searching for words.

"Aiden, you OK?"

"Yeah, I was just, I just got back from a walk. Mrs. Robinson thinks I'm sick, but I'm fine. What's up?"

"Are you sure? I can come get you."

"Seriously, I'm OK. What's up?"

"Oh... ah... I wanted to ask you something."

"Yeah?" *Geezus, just spit it out.*

"You... wanna spend the night? We can watch movies and eat cheese puffs and... who knows..." He went silent.

Something ached for me to hang up. What if Matte called me while I was on the phone, and I missed his call? I shook my head at the ridiculous thought. Of course, the phone would let me know if there was another call coming through.

"Aiden?" Harry called out.

"Oh sorry, yeah. That sounds great."

He sighed loudly.

"Oh, thank goodness. For a second, I thought you were going to reject me. I was like, *noooo,* inside. Do you need me to get you?"

"No, I can walk. I'll see you tonight."

"Okey doke."

156

The second I pulled the phone away from my ear, I saw the message icon. My heart jumped with excitement and nervousness. I hung up and tapped the messages app. Matte had texted back, "Hey."

I tapped on the enter message bar. The keyboard came up and so did another message from Matte. "So, what's up?" I fell right back in.

"Nothing much."

"You home?" he asked.

"Yes," I replied immediately. I wanted to tell him how much I missed him.

"I'll see you in a bit."

"Wait, you're coming here?"

No reply.

"Can't I just come by your place?" I asked.

No reply.

I looked at the time on the corner of the screen then down to the messages app then back up to the time. I walked back and forth in my room. I clicked on his name then backed out then checked the time again.

There was no reply for ten whole minutes.

"Here," he texted.

I didn't want Matte to be at my house. The unstable nature of it made my stomach hurt. I was afraid my father would show and destroy everything that I had created. But I had no choice, I couldn't turn him away. I needed to see him.

"The door is unlocked," I texted back.

I heard the front door open and footsteps on the way to my room. He peeked in the door and stared at me. My heart raced the second our eyes met. I motioned him to come in. He came in and closed the door, locking it behind him.

He was dressed so casually, very unlike him. His hair was messy. He wore a plain, white T-shirt and grey sweatpants. He looked tired and maybe a little sad. His eyes were puffy like he'd been crying. I instantly wondered if he had.

He sat on my bed and kicked his shoes off. They hit the floor hard. I sat on the nightstand waiting for him to say something. I needed to hear his voice.

"You've been hanging out with the priest?" he asked.

The question knocked me back, catching me off guard. I shook my head trying to make sense of how specific his question was. Out of every possible thing he could bring up, Harry was the last thing on the list.

"Harry?" I asked. His eyes widened as I spoke his name. "Yeah, he's my friend."

He sighed.

"Aiden, you have no friends. You hate people." His head cocked to one side, his face was plain, and his eyes were glued on me.

I didn't know what to say. His statement was true, and his tone almost hurtful.

"You guys fucking?" he asked, again shocking me.

"Wha..."

"Just tell me, dude."

"We are," I said as I stood up.

He was no longer surprised. He stared at me, sizing me down to the piece of shit I was. What did he expect? For me to lie to him, like he used to lie to me?

"That's good, I guess. I'm happy for you. He seems like a nice guy."

He threw his body back onto my bed. His shirt lifted up just enough for me to see a glimpse of skin.

Fuck, he knew that drove me crazy. He knew that made blood rush to my dick faster than anything ever could.

"Do you remember that concert we went to that one time?" he asked.

How could I forget, it was the best day of my life. I remembered the day perfectly. We walked the entire venue, stage by stage, holding hands. We didn't care if people saw us. We wanted them to see us. I wanted everyone to see me with this gorgeous man and know he was *all* mine.

"Do you remember when we got to the reservoir? That sunset? God, I play that in my head all the time. That entire day was the first time I ever saw the real you," he looked up at me. "It was the first time you let your walls down and allowed me to see you having fun. You didn't even wear your hoodie."

"I had you, I didn't need the hoodie."

Images of that night flooded my mind. We sat on the trunk of his car and watched the sunset. The sand around us glowed a vibrant red, and the air was cool enough for us to need each other's warmth. He put his arm around me, and I caved into his chest. And then we made love, under billions and billions of stars. Our love was timeless. It was the perfect ending to the already perfect day.

I stood from the nightstand. I walked up to him and kneeled at his feet. His heat radiated towards me reminding me that we'd been each other's many times before. Oh boy, I missed him. I reached out and rubbed his exposed abdomen carefully tracing his happy trail. I leaned my forehead against his knee and closed my eyes.

It was pointless to fight the natural course of our actions. We were a CD playing the same old song, skipping every part that allowed me free will. He was there for a reason, and I had already failed at holding my own before he even came into my house.

He sat up and ran his fingers through my messy hair. I looked up at him, and he looked down at me. He grabbed my face and pulled me in. We kissed hard, smacking our lips and gasping for air. He pulled his shirt off, and I stood up. He pulled my shorts and boxers down exposing my hard dick. He put it in his mouth and sucked. It was so warm and wet, I wanted to fucking explode.

I gripped at his bare back, digging my chewed nails in. He stopped and pulled me down to the bed. I had no control. I had surrendered it all to him, and he knew it. I was his all over again.

The next morning, I lay awake playing back everything that happened. My body ached, and my ass was sore. Matte's crisp, fresh scent was engraved on my skin, and our cum dried on the sheets. I rubbed my fingers on the moist, hardening spots on my bed, remembering his dick in me and the taste of his breath.

At some point during the night, I heard Matte get up. He stumbled in the dark, getting dressed before sneaking out the window. I fought against every desire to stop him. I didn't want him to leave, but I didn't want to beg him to stay.

I was lucky my father never came home. Having him find another man in my bed would've been the end of time. He would've killed us all, himself included.

The sun peered into the room and attempted to peel me off the bed. I didn't want the night to be over. I wanted to relive it again and again, memorize every detail so I could remember it for all eternity.

But it was all circles and triangles. Harry had called and texted multiple times. His texts went unanswered, and his voicemails left unheard. I couldn't bring myself to talk to him. I couldn't bear to hear his sadness. What I did was sick and undeniably selfish. Harry of all people didn't deserve that.

I threw my phone under the bed and covered my face with blankets. In my head, I was with Matte all over again.

The week that followed was interesting, to say the least. Matte and I continued to text briefly here and there. But our lives had drifted apart too much. An intimate encounter wasn't enough to glue us back together. He was different, even through text.

We talked about the weather. Summer was rapidly approaching, as well as his birthday and the anniversary of the day we met. We discussed plans, his mostly.

"Oh man, did I tell you Clarissa and I are going to see Escaping Fate?" he texted.

"Nah, I thought you didn't like that scremo shit?"

"I didn't, but Clarissa got me into them. They're pretty alright."

"Fuck, it's hot out there today. Oh, you know what? We should go to a water park for your birthday." I tried changing the subject.

"LOL, you're gonna get in the water with your hoodie on? But, I can't. Clarissa and I are going out for dinner."

"What about me? When do I get to see you?" I was starting to sound desperate.

"Dude, I talk to you more than I talk to anyone else. I'm sorry, I'm just busy."

It was pointless. Every time I tried to make plans with him, he undercut me by telling me he'd be doing this or that with Clarissa, always Clarissa. It was obvious that she was still around and wouldn't be going anywhere any time soon. She had taken over whatever was left of us and made it hers. Her existence sickened me, and the void it created widened with every breath.

I tried to distract myself with anything to help me forget. At the library, I frequented the computer room. The old degenerates masturbating under their tables helped kill time. I started busting them. At this point I had nothing to lose.

I'd come up from behind and rub their shoulders as they beat it. Some walked right out, but some surrendered their dicks to me. They let me stroke them there, in public. I still remember my hand wrapped around their dicks, my face so close I could nearly taste them. I'd jerk them off into a tissue and left with their semen in my pocket. Some would even follow me, to try and get more than just a hand job.

But I refused. My body belonged to someone else.

At my house I made an odd acquaintance. My single divorced neighbor, Bobby, began to lurk around when I was home alone. He was about my father's age, late forties. I knew he was into gay shit because of how he stared at me when I cut the lawn shirtless during my teenage years.

His eyes grew with me and he still stared even now when I walked by. So, I decided to give him a little more while helping me kill time.

One day I exposed myself "accidentally" in the living room's large bay window. I saw him come out the front door and walk to his mailbox. I sat on the couch with the curtains open. I wore a robe, but nothing else. He stood by the curb "looking' through mail across the street. I stood up and dropped the robe. He looked around then back into my window. I stroked my dick and walked out of view.

I don't know how, but the game quickly gained speed until I ended up masturbating in front of him almost daily. He loved when I dipped my balls in mayonnaise and jerked off with it in front of the open window. He lived for the final splat. It was oddly gratifying for me and, I'm sure, for him as well.

But, it wasn't enough. I wanted more. I wanted Matte.

I hadn't heard from Harry, and I wondered how he was. I looked at the last message he'd sent that night. I stared at the words on my phone screen and wondered how I could come back from that.

"I wish you would just talk to me," he had texted.

I was a sad piece of shit. There was no coming back from completely ghosting a friend. I felt bad. I felt really fucking bad, but I was sure it was no comparison to how Harry probably felt. I tapped on the phone icon and dialed his number.

The phone rang and rang. Each tone was long and dragged out. To my surprise, he picked up.

"Hello?" he said.

I hesitated for a second.

"Hey man," I said.

"What's up?" he asked.

"Harry, I'm really sorry for ditching you." I dove right in.

There was nothing but dead air for a solid minute.

"OK, is that it?" he asked.

"Dude, c'mon, don't do this." I tried to hold on.

"Aiden, what do you want me to say? I was worried sick about you. You didn't show, and you didn't text back or answer any of my calls. I drove by your house around midnight and *his car* was there. What do you expect me to say?"

This time I was the one who remained quiet. The way he said *his car* showed the full force of my actions. He knew I spent the night with Matte, so denying it would be worthless and lying cowardly.

"Listen Aiden, it's OK, though. I know we were just having fun. I... I wish... Thank you for showing me what I've been missing, really."

Abruptly, he hung up.

The days began bleeding into one another. Soon it was weeks since I last heard from both Harry and Matte. I never felt more alone. It was a constant battle to neglect the phone and avoid falling into the same old destructive patterns. Meaningless messages back and forth did nothing but create friction in every aspect of my life. The voices in my head screamed for Harry and yearned for Matte.

I felt stupid for wanting to be with Matte. He did nothing but yo-yo me around. I allowed him to ruin the only true friendship I ever had.

I began to miss work several times a week. I wasn't strong enough to be in the places that reminded me of them. The library was the center of their existence. I saw them at every corner. Mrs. Robinson talked about Harry as if he was the voice of the community. She talked him up so much, it made me sink lower.

Mrs. Cooper mentioned Matte's name in every conversation and regularly asked about him. Had I seen him during the weekend? Had we talked lately? How was he doing? They were all questions whose answers made my mouth bleed.

"No, sorry," was all I could say.

One evening, I slipped out the back door of the library like I used to do. I'd had enough of the townspeople for one day. The second I walked out, I noticed Harry leaning against his truck. He waited for me like Martia did every night for two years. He waited for me like I waited for Matte that one day.

"Hi Aiden," he said.

I was speechless. Sweat beaded on my forehead.

"Need a ride?"

"I need more than a ride." I held my arm across my chest like some sort of junkie.

"I know." He let out a crooked smile.

We got in his truck and sat silent for a moment. The air-conditioned cabin smelled like his cologne. It took me back to our fun days when everything was alright. It seemed so far away I looked at my feet. I couldn't bear to see him eye to eye. I felt him staring. The weight of everything pressed me against the seat and sealed my lips shut. My cheeks turned red. Sweat ran down my neck.

What could I say? Where could I even start?

"You probably know why I'm here." He said.

I shook my head.

"I can't live without you Aiden. I tried. I tried so hard, but I just can't get you out of my head."

I couldn't bear to see him.

What was I supposed to say? A lie -- that I felt the same way? Or the truth -- that I wanted him to replace Matte because he was actually there?

I just sat there, silently listening to us breathing.

"Say something. Please, Aiden, anything."

I looked at him now. He looked pathetic. His cheeks blushed, and his piercing blue eyes watered. This man wanted me more than he could want anything. I couldn't keep hurting him.

"I've missed you too." I said. It was the only true thing I could say that wouldn't hurt him anymore.

Harry talked the entire way to his house. I sat and listened as he described everything that he'd gone through the past few weeks.

"At first I was sad. I got home and I cried. I ate a whole tub of butter pecan ice cream and listened to the play list you sent me that one time. God, it was awful. But it reminded me of you. Who could I talk to? The ministers at church? No way. My mom? Forget about it. Not even Jesus answered when I prayed to him. And then you called. That only made me mad. I hated that piece of garbage."

He paused to make sure I was still listening. I continued staring at my feet.

"Then I was sad again. I tried reminding myself that I had no reason to be mad. I told myself that you weren't anything but a friend. It was so painful. So, I took a sabbatical and lay around my house. I couldn't get myself to do anything. I just wanted you back. Intercourse or no intercourse, I just wanted you to be there... next to me."

His feelings and his inability to conform to life without me were a clear reminder of how I felt about Matte. After everything that we had both been through, all I could think about was Matte. I looked at Harry and saw Matte's face. I heard Harry speak and all I could hear was Matte's voice. I loved Harry, but he wasn't my Jesus fucking Christ.

"I'm really fucking sorry, man. I didn't mean to hurt you." I was beginning to choke up.

"No, no, no, Aiden. Please don't. It's in the past. Let's leave it there."

I held back the tears and lowered my head as he put the truck in drive.

When we arrived at Harry's house, he was quiet. We stepped out the truck and walked up the pavers to the front door. Not much looked different. His hedges were trimmed, and his lawn was mowed. Once inside, the pristine nature of his home continued. Not a dust bunny in sight or couch cushion out of place.

Leave it to Harry to keep it together even when he's falling apart.

I sat on the couch, and Harry brought me a glass of water. He sat next to me and put his arm on my shoulders. He wasted no

164

time. He leaned in and threw his tongue in my mouth, his breath a bit sour. These were different kisses, they were hard and forced.

His hands were up and down my body. He grabbed my balls and squeezed them. He had never done that. I pulled away from his mouth, and he pulled my face to his again. He moved down my neck and sucked hard. I knew each one would bruise.

"Let's go to the bedroom," he whispered.

He stood and pulled me up. He seemed rushed and anxious. He pulled me to his bedroom and closed the door. He looked at his phone and put on the familiar playlist. I sat on his bed and pulled my shirt off. He sat next to me and sucked my neck some more between heavy gasps. I lay down and pulled my pants and boxers off while he did the same. I got a glance at his penis, already hard, as he got on top me. He continued to suck my neck then moved down to my chest.

Why was he being so rough? This wasn't like any other time. He'd always been timid and gone with my flow.

Harry lifted my legs over his shoulders. He spit on his hand and rubbed it on his dick. Without testing it out he jammed it in me. He continued sucking my chest harder and harder while pounding my ass raw. He gripped my ass cheeks and spread them wider. I imagined it ripping and spewing blood all over his clean sheets.

I pushed him gently, to get him to slow down but he didn't.

"I love you so much," he said in between sucks and thrusts.

I looked away while my eyes turned to liquid.

"Stop," I whispered.

He didn't.

I glanced back at Harry hoping to see Matte's face. But I didn't.

"Stop it, you're hurting me!"

Harry stopped sucking my neck and examined my face. Sobbing uncontrollably, I wiped my eyes and pushed him off me. I jumped off the bed and looked around for my clothes.

"Aiden, what's wrong?"

"I have to go. I can't be here. I have to talk to Matte. I have to find Matte."

"What do you mean?" He sat naked on the edge of the bed.

"I need to see Matte," I said looking straight at him.

"Why, Aiden? Why?" He punched the bed. "Matte will never love you the way you love him."

I stared at him in disbelief. He didn't know what we had. He didn't know the value of everything we had, regardless of time and distance. It was impossible for an outsider to see that.

"Aiden, don't you see? He is just using you. He has been using you all along. How much longer are you going to keep this charade going? Honestly. How much longer are you going to keep lying to yourself and keep waiting for something that will never come your way?"

I remained silent as I got dressed in the dim light. A tune played softly from Harry's phone, barely audible. It was mine and Matte's song.

"You're a fool. That's all you've ever been, a fool. You've never been anything more than an object for him. He will never love you. Matte will never love you the way I love you."

There was a moment of silence. I put on my shoes and walked to the door.

"If that's the case, then you should know I will never love you the way you love me."

Chapter 19

The days that followed rapidly declined. My nightmares returned, more violent and vivid than before. My uncle lived in them, making sure I didn't forget. Every day I woke up feeling like I was one more day overdue for death. I went through the days without a purpose. There was no reason for my existence. I had nothing to live for. I felt like I should have died a long time ago, before life got so hard, before my entire being revolved around *some dude*.

But it was too late. I was in too deep. Going back to try to fix everything would only make things worse. I had chosen to live the life my mistakes created for me, even if I had done so subconsciously.

That morning, as my eyes caught the first glimpse of sunlight, I wondered how much longer I would have to repeat the cycle of misery. Days were all the same, they followed a script that had been written long before I was even born. They mashed and blended together like some sort of fucked up painting, one that always felt like something was missing.

I lay awake on my bed, staring at the ceiling. The cracks on the stucco glared down at me. They were more than just the wrinkles of the shack's tired life. They were scars filled with hundreds and thousands of tiny people watching, waiting for my next move. They enjoyed my attempts to live and rejoiced when I failed.

I grabbed my dick and beat it savagely while forcing myself to null the pleasure it brought. I wasn't allowed to have pleasure, to have fun, or to be happy. Every time I did, something went horribly wrong. Just like every morning, I collected the ejaculate from my chest and filled the cracks on the ceiling with it.

I didn't even bother cleaning myself anymore. I got up from bed. Sweat and filth glued the sheets to my skin making it hard to peel them off. Dirty clothes littered the floor with small piles. I considered getting dressed but what was the point? I wasn't going anywhere. I lived in my room, surrounded by four walls in an ocean of thoughts.

I hadn't seen any of my family in a while. By the time I awoke, they were all gone for the day. I was beginning to forget their faces and their voices. My entire life was stuck in a place in time where they couldn't exist.

It had been weeks since the last time I set foot in the library. My job was gone. But that was OK. No one there ever gave a crap about me. I never took the time to get to know them. I never opened up to any of them. For all they knew, I was dead in a ditch somewhere.

I walked to the bathroom nude. Watery jizz raced to the floor leaving behind glistening trails. I stood over the toilet staring down at my body. Ribs pushed out behind my skin and my knees cracked, threatening to give way. Dark piss trickled out of me. It hit the walls of the toilet leaving marks against the white porcelain. The smell stung my nostrils, turning my eyes to liquid.

I washed my hands and splashed water on my face. The mirror couldn't bear the sight of me. My reflection stared at me as I stumbled away.

The empty house was dark and grey with unwanted memories of my dreaded life. Flashes of my youth were splattered on the walls, not a smile to be seen. I was so young and naïve, afraid of my own shadow. My uncles face peered through my eyes in every one of those photos.

I saw the ghosts of my brother and me in his room while my parents fought. I remembered taking him out the back door, so he wouldn't hear my father beat my mother.

"Where are we going?" he asked every time.

"Up, up, and away," I told him.

He smiled and skipped outside. I tried to shield him from anything that could hurt him. I was solely responsible for his sanity. It was a responsibility that I could no longer keep.

Memories of past girlfriends lived around every corner. I'd been nothing but an object to them. I lived the life they wanted me to live: fuck and get high. There were never feelings. There was never any sharing of life moments. We never grew as partners nor individuals. We never even knew each other. I was their dick, and they were my drugs.

The floorboards recounted memories of my loneliness. Each creak told the story of how I hid in the darkness of my room trying to forget how fucked up life was. Each squeak reminded me how day after day was nothing more than a waiting game for something good to happen.

I never understood why it had to be so hard to stay alive and why we had to. Why were my mother, brother, and I prisoners of a life so shitty? Why were we brought to life just to suffer... what was the point of it all?

Then there were memories of him... Matte Black. How wonderful the beginning of it was and how different from all my other relationships it had become. I was eager to start a new day just to see him. We got lost in each other's eyes every time we'd lie in each other's arms... and I felt alive. When I was with him, I was alive.

He made me believe he would always be there for me, and I trusted him. I trusted him so much that I allowed him to take control of my life. I allowed him to destroy the only real friendship I ever had, Harry.

I missed Harry. He was an angel in a human body, and I was the demon who destroyed him. I was no better than Matte. I wanted to make it right but every attempt I made was blocked by my inability to function as a normal human being. I walked out his door and didn't look back.

Those were the most painful memories to keep. When life finally had a purpose and how that purpose eventually destroyed me.

I sat around the house waiting for someone to knock on the door, for anyone to message my phone. I waited for something to happen, to show me why I was still alive. My days were wasting away. *I* was wasting away.

It was exactly a year ago when Matte and I officially met. It had been a 365-day rollercoaster from which I couldn't get off.

The ups and downs of it gave me whiplash. I would never forget May 8th, the day I unknowingly began my journey through the walkways of a slaughterhouse to my final destination. I was a helpless creature in a hopeless world.

My heart ached. Every beat sent oxygen to my brain to feed the constant stream of toxic memories. My head wanted to explode. Nothing other than Matte existed within the walls of my skull. He had taken over my body and mind. All I thought about was him and if he ever thought about me. I wondered if I crossed his mind the way he did mine. Of course, I didn't. I never had. I was always the last thing he worried about in his life, at best.

Why didn't he love me? Why couldn't I let him... go?

It was supposed to be more than just a summer fling. It was supposed to last more than just a few fucks. But I was never more than a short expansion of his exploration. With one word, he made me feel higher than any drug ever did only to tear me down and destroy me with another. And now, all I had were memories, black and white pictures of what I thought we had.

What I thought we had... we never had anything.

I spent hours every day staring at the dark screen of my phone waiting for it to come to life with his name.

His. God. Damned. Name.

I was even in love with his fucking name. How does that even happen? I was so infatuated with him, with us, with the idea of us.

After a few hours I fought against my will to pick up the phone and wake it from its slumber. I opened the messages and stared at his picture. The restroom selfie stared back at me. The picture he took when we were new to each other, and the future was a story waiting to be written. The picture that I would stare at every time I got high. That picture would haunt me for the rest of my life.

But now that day was but a distant memory. It had been weeks since I last heard from him, and the distance was killing me. I wasn't strong enough to live without him, and he knew it. He fed off the idea of me living at the snap of his fingers. Although he was never mine, I was always his.

I clicked on him and began to type. I wrote the words I wanted to scream to his face. I typed paragraphs full of emotions

170

that went from love to rage and finally dwindled to apologies. I was sorry for disturbing him, for wanting us to be in each other's lives. I wanted him to know what and how I felt, for him and for everything that was happening. I needed him to know how much he meant to me and how much it hurt that he'd pushed me aside.

But I knew more than likely he wouldn't even read my messages. I knew I wasn't even worth a second of his time. He had made that clear time and time again.

I stood there for a minute staring into the phone, into our past... into my past. No one had ever cared like he had and now it seemed like he didn't either. I had no one. I was alone, naked, and broken in a world that existed only in my head.

I woke the phone back up and deleted every written character.

At a loss for words, I typed his signature phrase "So what's up?" and pressed send.

My eyes shut and I fell into the void of his absence, where I floated around with images of us.

He replied an hour later, "Can't talk now... hanging out with Clarissa."

I gasped as, for a second I felt hope, relief at the fact that just for a few moments in time I was in his mind even if I had put myself there. But that quickly turned to angst.

Why did I always have to be the one who reached out? Why was I the only one who was trying? Love doesn't work that way. You don't put yourself in the mind of the person that's supposed to love you. You are supposed to be that person's entire life.

"Fuck you! Fuck you, you fucking faggot!! I... I fucking love you!" I screamed at the phone.

Tears rushed down my face as my throat twisted in knots that would never come undone. I wanted him. I wanted to be part of his life, not part of his lie. It didn't matter how long I held on. He was simply turning into just *some guy I used to fuck*. But did it matter? Did any of it even matter? We're born alone, and we're destined to die alone.

I gripped the phone in my hand and clenched my teeth. I was tired of trying. I was exhausted. I was so stupid to fall for someone so selfish.

But mostly, I was angry.

I was furious at myself for allowing things to get that far. Why couldn't I accept that I was just the side piece? He would never leave Clarissa for me. To her and to everyone we encountered, I would never be anything more than just his *buddy Aiden*.

Love is way too hard.

I shut my eyes and fell to the floor. Whatever was left of me pushed tears out through my closed lids. They trickled down my face and splashed on my thighs. There was nothing more I could give.

I opened my eyes and ran out of my bedroom. I barged into my mother's room and rummaged through her nightstand drawers. If Matte wouldn't bail me out, drugs would. I took a handful of Prozac. Then, I took one of my father's half empty beers from the floor and gulped everything down.

I wobbled back to my room and closed the door, locking it behind me. I placed some strips on my tongue, more than I could count. I wanted to forget everything. I needed to forget him.

My phone went off, but I ignored it.

"I wish we would have never locked eyes..." I whispered.

My phone continued to beg for my attention.

"I wish we would have never heard each other's voices..." I whispered.

The voicemails piled up.

"I... wish... I would have never loved you..." I cried.

The walls bled from the ceiling, and the floor around me cracked. I had to get out before I fell. I struggled to unlock the door as my fingers dissolved again and again. I succeeded only after licking them. I opened the door to find stairs that led to darkness. Unsure if I could walk them, I threw myself on the floor and dropped my phone. I frantically searched for it, but it was gone.

I looked in my backpack and found cocaine. I dumped the baggie into my palm, pressed my face onto the maggots, and inhaled. The larvae dripped from my nose and disintegrated at the sight of the flames creeping through the cracks.

My eyes opened wide; I smelled sulfur. I was going to hell.

"Matte! Matte!" I called for him.

"I love you Matte!" I cried for him.

Smoke rose from the cracks and mixed with the endless flow of blood from the walls, creating a slurry, thick and suffocating.

I knew I was going to die.

"Aiden… Aiden, honey, get up…" my mother called out.

She used the same tone when she begged my father to stop beating her.

I waved my arms through the smoke but couldn't find her. The flames charred my skin. I dug my fingers in, pulling chunks off.

"Mom! Why doesn't he love me, Mom? Why doesn't he love me?"

"Baby, what's wrong sweetheart?"

My mother stood before me wearing her Sunday dress, frayed and dirty. She stood perfectly still, her face erased from her head.

"Aiden, please get up! How can you do this to me?"

"Why does he hurt me, Mom? Please make it stop, Mommy."

I was tired of the pain.

I heard my brother in the distance.

"Aiden! Brother!" Get up, Aiden; what's wrong?"

It pained me to hear them like that. Why did I always have to make them cry, make them suffer just like my father did? I was no better than him.

The smoke, blood, and slurry whirled around me. The faceless statues of my mother and brother stood before me and watched me go. They faded in and out with small gaps of silence and grief. I was sorry for making them witness my death. I was sorry for being a failure.

But it was too late. My body was cemented. My feet branched onto the wood planks of the floor, becoming part of them. My body decayed as my sins ate me away.

"How can you do this to me Aiden? How?"

Chapter 20

I never told anyone. They wouldn't understand.

They wouldn't feel his hands on my body or his breath on my skin. They wouldn't feel the deep wounds that he carved throughout my insides every time it happened.

I knew my mother often wondered what was bottled inside my head. She combed my hair and dressed me. She cooked me meals and fed me. She stared into my eyes, but she couldn't see through them. She watched me grow without ever growing older.

I always knew I was different. I wasn't a normal child. I wasn't a happy child. No matter what my mother tried, the clouds above me never gave way to sunshine. Some people are broken beyond repair. Not even the glue of love can repair the cracks that lust creates.

When we're young, we view the world with curious eyes. We make mistakes and learn from them. We run through the days, taking everything in. We marvel at the vibrant colors of nature and wonder at its beauty.

Personally, I loved baby watermelons. It felt great to know that I, at seven years old, could create life with simple gardening. But it was nothing compared to the feeling of crushing their tiny structures with my foot. The inner make-up of the fruit simply fascinated me.

My grandmother watched me throughout most of my childhood. She taught me what my parents were incapable of, the basics of life. She showed me how to garden. She showed me how to bathe and clothe myself, for when my parents weren't around. She showed me how to bake a vast variety of baked goods. Her house always smelled like cookies, and her hugs were always warm.

My mother worked hard and was rarely around to watch me grow. That's what poor people do; they get screwed with a family they can't afford, and then they spend their lives working to provide for the kids they wish they didn't have. So, while my mother was busy providing for my father's addictions, my grandmother raised me as well as she could.

But her aging eyes couldn't be everywhere.

Words can't fully explain the trauma and pain certain actions create. No one ever stops and thinks, "Oh that's how it all started." No, I can't even recall the amount of times I tried to justify it in my head. The many times I lied to myself and told myself that it was my fault, that if only I hadn't done this or said that, then maybe *he* wouldn't have done *it*. But there are only so many places in my head that I can hide the days, to try to erase his ways.

It was an accident the first time I saw his dick. My uncle walked around the house in nothing other than his old, white, nearly transparent, boxers. The stains and holes on them told the tales of his actions. Although he always did it, I never paid attention until that day.

"Why in the world do you keep doing this?!" my grandmother asked. "Look at this mess. They're all ruined!"

I sat at the kitchen table as my grandmother scolded me for destroying her crops, again. She took her hat off and threw it on the floor next to me.

"Now, because of you, we're not going to have watermelons this summer. Your uncle loves watermelon! Do you know how much they cost at the store? I cannot believe this. I should've never shown you the tiny fruit. I thought you would like seeing it grow before your eyes. Boy, I was wrong. Never, never again!"

She yelled and waved her hands as she walked in circles around the kitchen. Pieces of fruit flew and hit the wall behind me.

The entire time she screamed, I looked past her to her son, the twenty-year old loser who stood a few feet behind her. Every time he moved, the bulge in his boxers jiggled. He stretched for a second and the fly of his boxers opened, exposing his privates. I was enchanted.

"For heaven's sake, are you even listening to a word I'm saying? Aiden? Aiden!"

I broke the trance and looked at my grandmother's sharp grey eyes. There was no explanation for what I had done except for the truth.

"I hate the way they look. They're so fuzzy."

I was talking about the tiny watermelons, but I guess the response could have applied to my uncle's balls just as well.

"Jesus... forget it. I don't know what I'm gonna do with you, boy."

She threw the crushed, muddy corpses in the trash, and left the room, allowing my life to take a darkened path.

"What you looking at pussy?" my uncle said, flipping me off. "Huh? Huh, pussy? You lookin' at my dick? You like that shit?"

He quickly pulled his dick out of his underwear, shaking it inches from my face.

I couldn't speak. Aside from print, I had never seen another penis in my life, especially not one that large. How easy it is to ruin a child's innocence.

"You like that? Huh, pussy?"

He smacked my cheeks with his growing erection over and over. When I closed my eyes, he smacked my glasses, leaving dirty smudges on them.

"You like the way that smells? Huh? Just wait till you see how it tastes..."

I heard my grandmother's flip-flops, flopping back towards the kitchen. In my little boy mind, I begged for her to walk faster. I wanted her to catch him in the act. She was my teacher, my guardian, his mother. She was the one who could stop him, the hero I needed. But before she could, my uncle stopped. I opened my eyes as he pulled his penis back into his boxers. I looked at the kitchen doorway, and my uncle snuck away into his bedroom.

From that day forward, the occurrences only grew more explicit. Over time, he grew more comfortable exposing himself to me, and what started off as. what I assumed was a game, quickly turned into something darker.

Some days, he waited by the doorway of his bedroom as my mother dropped me off in the morning. He wouldn't say a word, he simply stood there in his underwear, watching me. He stared as I ate, played, bathed, and slept. He wouldn't talk. He just watched. Those were the good days, when he didn't touch me.

On days when my grandmother went to the store or to her friend's house next door, *God* must have forgotten I was alive.

"Let's play a game," he would say. "C'mon get under the covers."

He waited for my little hands to lift the covers and discover his naked body. I didn't want to see him like that. I didn't want to see his penis swollen with desire. But I had no choice. He was the grown up, and I was under his *care*.

"Grab it," he said.

I shrank back.

"Like this," he said as he grasped my hand and placed it on his dick.

My hands were barely big enough to wrap around it. I couldn't fight back the tears. I sobbed uncontrollably. But that was pointless. Crying wouldn't make him stop.

After the *playful* wrestling matches under the covers, he would sit on the edge of his bed, his erection throbbing furiously, waiting for my young mouth.

"C'mon... c'mon... you know what to do..." he would say.

Refusing to do it, he did it for me. He killed a little part of me every time he forced himself into me.

It never got easier. It hurt every time. And the pain grew with me.

After every time he rearranged my insides, he sat me on the floor. With his calloused hands, he rubbed my eyes and lips, wiping away the tears and jizz. After every occurrence, he repeated the same words like a spell to protect his sorry ass.

"You're not going to tell your Mom, are you? You're not going to tell your Dad, are you? You're not going to tell your Grandma, are you?"

He went down the list of people, pausing for my response. After my silent *no,* he continued to the next known person. I always hoped he forgot to mention someone, anyone so I could tell them and get the torture over with. But he never did. He knew exactly what he was doing. I was never safe. I was his prey everywhere I went, and he was my shadow, even on the darkest days.

It was rare to find a moment of joy even at my own house. I expected to see him sitting in the kitchen, drinking coffee. I expected to see him behind the shower curtain when I took a poo. I expected to see him lurking in the hallways of my house, wearing nothing but his worn out boxers.

One day, all I wanted to do was go outside and plant some watermelons. I wanted to relive more innocent times. With a pocket full of seeds and a day full of sunshine, I left my room. As I strolled down the hall, my father came out of the bathroom, wearing only a towel. He paused to sip his beer when the towel accidentally dropped.

I froze and lost control of my emotions.

"No, no, no... no... no!" Piss ran down my legs and puddled at my feet.

My father glared at me.

"Oh, you son of a bitch, what did you do?!" he screamed and stomped towards me still naked.

"No please don't."

I closed my eyes, and pain followed.

My father slapped me across the face, knocking me to the ground and sending my glasses flying across the hall. Heat and numbness spread throughout my face. My eyes watered uncontrollably. I bit my tongue hard so I wouldn't make a sound. I didn't want to make it worse. Screaming always made everything worse.

"Clean this shit up right now!"

I did.

Through my blindness, I grabbed paper towels from the kitchen to clean my panicked mess. I wiped everywhere I could see. I threw the soaked towels in the trashed and picked up my glasses. I walked silently back to my bedroom and shut the door. I threw myself on the bed and attempted to straighten my glasses. The frame was bent to a point where they wouldn't sit straight on my face. I took them off and never wore them again. I was embarrassed people would see the reasons behind their crooked ways.

I always wondered if telling him would make him feel sorry and offer me comfort. On most days that's all I really needed, a strong father to protect me from the man who stole my innocence. I doubt it. He probably would've blamed me. He was never there for me. Instead he called me a queer every time I did something wrong.

A queer... it was as if he knew before I did.

My uncle continued his games for the following five years of my life. My body changed and so did its innate responses. My uncle's games grew with me. They escalated to fulfill his thrills. Every chance he got, he wrote my future and carved his name on my young body.

I eventually entered my teens and didn't need much supervision. Broken or not, we all grow older. My thirteenth year on this Earth marked yet another beginning in my miserable life.

Not much mattered anymore. My world had lost its color. I found no interest in gardening. My favorite TV shows and movies no longer held my attention. They were just moving pictures without context.

Each year had gotten a little darker.

Still, I had somehow managed to make friends, normal friends. Ben, Tyler, Jacob, and I became friends over summer break before eighth grade. These were kids that I grew up with, classmates I never cared for, and somehow, we bonded over a dead cat. They thought it was cool when I picked it up off the road and tossed it over into someone's yard. They were complete idiots, and we became inseparable.

We spent nearly every day of that summer together. We swam in Ben's swimming pool during the hot days, and we had bonfires and sleepovers at Tyler's during the nights.

It seemed that through the darkness, life was finally taking a right turn. We talked about everything; school, girls, cars, parents, and a new discovery... jerking off. I was already too familiar with it, unfortunately.

We spent the night at Tyler's house more often than anyone else's for two reasons: he had no siblings who could disturb us, and the vacant upstairs bedroom was in perfect view into the neighbors' abnormally large bathroom window. I can't even recall how we came upon that miracle. All I know is one night while watching Spider-Man, he blurted out, "You guys, let's go upstairs."

The upstairs bedroom had been vacant since his Grandmother passed away a few years prior. Now, it served one purpose, voyeurism.

We waited in the dark for nearly twenty minutes as Tyler tried to silence our giggles every five seconds.

"Man, this is boring. What are we even waiting for?" Ben asked.

"Shh... hold up..." Tyler looked at his watch and adjusted his *bulge*.

Not a minute later, the room dimly lit with the neighbor's bathroom light. Tyler ordered us to gather around the window and crouch under the sill. We looked out through the blinds into the neighboring oversized window.

A young lady looked at herself in the mirror briefly. She tied her long black hair into a bun before running her hands down her neck, and then cupping her breasts. She peeled her tank-top off and slid out of her shorts. She stepped into the shower and turned the water on. I had never seen my friends as silent and still as they sat that night.

The window provided a full view of the female's body. It wasn't the first time I had seen a naked woman. I had run into some of my father's magazines several times before. You know, just another part of my unprotected childhood.

We continued to watch the young woman as she caressed her body with the steaming water. It was delicate and seductive. We watched her lather up before steam blurred the glass shower door.

"Check this out," Tyler said, dropping his shorts.

He grabbed his already erect penis and began to stroke. Ben and Jacob looked at each other, and then at me before asking him, "Whatcha doin?" We pretended not to know what he was doing.

"Try it guys. It feels amazing," he replied.

Our growing bulges begged for attention. Ben and Jacob followed Tyler's example. I stood back and watched a little freaked out... a little aroused. They all looked at me and egged on

180

to do it. It felt wrong, it felt like a violation of their privacy. It was the first time I had ever seen my friend's dicks and I... I kinda liked it. I hesitantly took out my dick and joined in behind them.

Tyler moved on to the bed, placed his erection between the mattresses and began to thrust. The boys continued to watch out the window while I watched *them*. The sweat beading on their foreheads, their quick and short strokes, the wet noises, their heavy breathing... it was almost too much for me to handle.

I stroked along with them, slow at first, then faster and faster. It felt wrong, but good. It was exciting and arousing in many different ways. I couldn't stop staring.

It wasn't long before the wave of orgasms began; first Ben, then Jacob, next Tyler and finally me. The strange but all too familiar scent of semen filled the room. It wasn't awkward or weird. It seemed normal for us to do together what we probably already did in private.

"Here, use this..." Tyler said throwing a toilet paper roll at Ben.

He passed it around so the rest of us could clean up our own messes. Ben threw his dirty tissue at Jacob. Jacob dodged it and threw his back at Ben. Tyler laughed as he wiped the tip of his penis, and then threw his tissue at me. I caught it in midair and squished it in my hand. Globs of jizz protruded between my fingers. They all laughed and ran out the room.

I stared at my sticky hand before something out the window caught my eye. I looked into the neighbor's bathroom window and saw the young woman look into our room and smile satisfied, that she had given us our hoped-for show. I looked to see if any of the guys saw her do that, but they were gone. None of my friends saw what I saw.

We continued jerking off together nearly every Friday night. My friends watched the neighbor, and I watched them. They never knew. The feeling of watching them brought a whole new meaning to the naked male body. It was different than watching my uncle.

It was now clear in my mind that I was attracted to guys instead of girls. At first, I thought it was my uncle's fault, but then I realized that it wasn't. I had felt that attraction before his games began. I used to look at the men in my father's nudy magazines. I was always more mesmerized by men more than by the women. The feelings were confusing. I was confused. They were feelings that I couldn't understand and struggled to accept.

I remember the next bump on the road of my life clearly. One night while we waited for the young woman to make an appearance, her boyfriend walked in instead of her. He was lean and scruffy. His brown hair was shaggy and messy. I liked it.

My friends groaned and left the room, erect and disappointed. I stayed behind.

I couldn't get my eyes off the shirtless guy in the neighboring bathroom. He looked at himself in the mirror and poked at his face. He turned the shower on and unbuttoned his jeans. He took a digital camera out of his pocket and took a quick selfie, with the camera up high looking down to his abs and undone pants. He set the camera on the counter and took his pants and black boxer-briefs off before jumping in the shower. Fuck. This was the show *I* had been waiting for, the show *I* wanted explode to.

I grabbed my dick and beat it wildly. I stared at his face for a second before nervously making my way down. I loved the way his hair looked wet. I loved how water dripped down his body; around his arms, down his chest, over his abs, his ass, his... dick.

It was perfect.

After I came, I lingered in the dark silent bedroom for a moment. I felt guilty and dirty. My semen lay as a string on the floor ahead of me. What was I turning into? Some sort of sick freak like... *him*? I was going to turn into the man I hated the most and there wasn't shit I could do about it. The guilt tore me from within. I stuffed my penis back in my shorts and looked at the empty room before me.

To the unknowing eye, the bedroom was a simple furnished room, but to me it was more than that. It was a milestone in my life, unfortunately not a good one. I looked around remembering where each of my friends did their deed. When I got to the right corner of the bed I paused, remembering Tyler plunging his erection between the mattresses. He never really used his hands for it. He refused to. He always said, "If jizz touches your hand, that means you're gay."

182

I always found his masturbatory habits oddly arousing.

I kneeled on the floor and lifted the mattress. Between the top mattress and the lower plastic covered box spring lay his dry seed. I looked at it, contemplating what I should do.

I didn't want to be gay. I didn't want to feel the way I did. I didn't want to do the things I did.

I closed my eyes and ran my fingers over it feeling the crusty ripples created by the plastic wrapping. I opened my eyes and watched the dry flakes on my fingers. They sparkled like broken glass with the soft light that came in through the open blinds. I had to keep them. I wanted to keep a bit of him with me, as messed up as it sounded in my head. After careful deliberation, I wiped my fingers in my pockets and left the room, satisfied but heavy.

I continued to watch the young woman's boyfriend's shower routines for several weeks. It was every Friday at 11 p.m., forty-five minutes after she showered. My friends never knew where I was or what I was up to. They'd gone to bed after the show the girl put on for us.

But my thirst kept getting stronger. I wanted to get as close as I could, close enough to feel his pubes brushing against my cheeks.

So, one day I did the unthinkable.

I snuck out the back door. In the darkness of the night, I jumped the fence and climbed the lattice on the side of the house onto their roof. I crawled on the roof tiles to their abnormally large bathroom window.

Why was that window so big? It was almost as if the architects who designed it, did it with voyeurism in mind.

I peeked inside and waited for him to walk in. After a few minutes of waiting, my erection became too uncomfortable for my underwear. I pulled it out and began to stroke, hoping he would walk in soon. I don't know what I was thinking. I was a stupid child, just waiting to get caught in a dirty perverse act.

A few minutes later, the door swung open, and the light went on. To my dismay, the young woman walked in and caught me jerking off right outside her bathroom window. I hadn't crouched enough to hide.

She wasn't scared or startled. She expected me. I didn't expect what was about to happen.

"Hmm... my, my, look at you." She didn't hesitate. "We finally meet. Haha."

I gulped hard, frightened.

"Come here, show me what you can do with that..." she said, pulling me in through the open window.

My heart was racing, and my erection throbbed. She grabbed a hold of it. My penis looked different in her hand. Her long red nails lightly traced the head making a dot of precum pop out. She looked at me with her piercing hazel eyes. She licked her lips and kneeled to take it in her mouth. It was wet and warm. She pulled it out and traced the dick hole with her tongue piercing. It felt wrong. It felt good, but wrong.

She moaned and took it all in again, balls deep. I didn't want her, I wanted her man. I wanted her to stop sucking. I wanted her to stop moaning. I wanted to stop enjoying it. I couldn't stop her. I couldn't stop... until I came.

She swallowed every drop of me. Her bright red lips formed a smile. She could pass for innocent. The devil certainly has many disguises.

"Good boy," she said. "Now go on before Russel comes up."

She kissed my cheek and squeezed my ass. She lightly pushed me towards the open window, rubbing her fingers up and down my back. I put my deflating penis away, zipped up my pants, and climbed out the window.

I shook the entire way home. I couldn't go back into the sleepover. I didn't want my friends to know what had just happened. Nobody could know what she had done. I went home... to my room... to my closet.

I should have never gone back, to Tyler's, to the rooftop to try and see *her* boyfriend. But I did. And every time I went back, she waited for me. She pulled me into the bathroom and had her way with me. She sucked me and kissed me. Sometimes she made me shower with her. She sat me on the tiled shower floor and rode my dick raw. She rubbed her breasts all over my face as she pulled my hair back. She sucked hard bruises onto my neck and chest. She claimed me as hers.

I hated myself. I hated my uncle, and I hated her. I hated my disgusting body. I hated that my dick always did what *they* wanted it to do. It was no longer my body.

I couldn't believe I was turning into another object for a different person. What did I ever do to deserve that? Was that God's way of showing me that I wasn't supposed to like men? Was God even real? Or was He just a name some pedophile came up with to scream out every time he'd fuck his victims?

"Oh God... Oh God... Oh God..."

After a few months I stopped spending the night at Tyler's. I ghosted my friends without explanation. They didn't ask, and I never told. We just simply fell apart as many friends do.

But for the next three years, I continued to see Kat every Friday at midnight. I wasn't sure if it was because I wanted to feel something or because I never felt anything. She had managed to push the thoughts of naked men and the feelings I had towards them back into the depths of my mind. She replaced them with the reality of pleasuring a woman... breasts, pussy, and orgasms.

That's what boys, men, are supposed to like... right? That was normal, right? I... was normal, right?

I started distancing myself from the world around me. I didn't fit in anywhere. I spent time only with myself and my thoughts. No one could understand me. Life was easier when I didn't have to explain why I was so quiet and weird.

A few days after my sixteenth birthday I sat alone by the train tracks behind the high school, lost in thought as I often was. The years pressed down, heavy on my body and mind. My soul was old. The wrinkles of abuse made me older than I really was. I had turned into the loser I was destined to be. I had no friends. I couldn't keep them. I had no direction. I was never given one. I was alone, always alone.

A girl in my school came up behind me. I didn't know her name. I had seen her in the hallways several times but had never spoken to her. She always dressed in black. Her hair was always different colors, and the fresh cuts on her arms were always covered with bracelets and ribbons. There was always something about her that caught my attention, something that attracted me and pulled me in.

She sat on the tracks next to me and stared at the darkening horizon with me.

"Looks like you could use some help," she said.

Her voice was strong but pained. I didn't reply. I couldn't, I didn't know how to talk to strangers. All I knew how to do was *fuck.*

But she was right, I did need help. I had reached the end of the line and wasn't sure if I could keep going. I felt the strong urge to scream everything to her, sparing no details. I wanted to tell her that the last nine years of my life had been a living, fire-induced nightmare, and that I was ready for it to be over. But I didn't. I swallowed my words and held back the tears like the *good boy* I was taught to be.

She reached into her backpack, and then extended her arm towards me. She opened her fist and revealed a handful of white pills.

"This helps," she said.

I glanced at her green eyes then at the pills. I needed to forget.

"Take some," she ordered.

I took the pills and threw them in my mouth gulping without the help of water. Every pill I downed hurt just as much as every memory I hoped to forget.

"Let's fuck," she ordered.

I never had a choice.

Chapter 21

My eyes opened to a dark room.

For a moment I didn't know if I was dead or still alive. It's sad when you don't even know the difference between the two. The popcorn ceiling above me glowed in the dim light. I looked around the room trying to familiarize myself with my surroundings. The shadows on the walls went from my escaped demons back to ordinary objects.

As usual Matte jumped into my head. He was often the first thing on my mind even before I knew who or where I was. I wasn't dead. Of course not. Giant sacks of shit like myself never died. My father was living proof of that. We were like a virus, spreading, causing pain, and suffering to those closest to us.

In the corner of the room, my mother slouched on a chair. She looked old and frail, tired of life and tired of the same crap. I felt sorry for her. I was a disappointment like her father, like my father, like all the men she'd ever held dear. Her life was shit, like theirs, and like mine.

The day she told me she was pregnant with my brother popped into my head.

She sat me on the edge of the bed and put her hand on my leg. She fought back the tears for as long as she could. Breaking down, she told me, "I'm pregnant... you're going to have a little brother."

"Why are you crying?" I asked, confused as I always thought babies made people happy.

"I don't want him to live like this..." She rubbed my leg. Tears rushed down her cheeks. "He deserves better."

I knew exactly what she meant. We were poor in every sense of the word. We hadn't seen my father in days; we had no money, no food, and we lived in borderline squalor. I was only fourteen years old, and I knew that wasn't the life anybody should have to live.

I never got used to the pain and suffering.

"Mom?" I called out. My voice was coarse and dry. I rarely ever called her mom. To me she had always been Mother.

"Aiden! Brother! Mom, he's up," my little brother screamed.

He had been sleeping on the extra bed in the room. I hadn't even noticed his presence.

"Aiden, heavens, don't move," she ordered.

I then noticed the restraints that bound me to the bed. I had needles and tubes in my arms and legs, and my throat ached. I couldn't feel my nose, and my stomach twisted and turned. The reality of my mistakes settled in.

My mother ran out the door calling for a doctor's attention before rushing back in. She had dark bags under her red eyes, her skin was blotchy, her clothes were wrinkly, and her hair was pulled back in a messy ponytail. She looked older than she really was.

All of it was my fault.

"Aiden, why... why did you do this to yourself? Why did you do this to me, to us?" She held one hand to her chest and pointed the other at my brother.

She looked like she was about to cry, but her eyes were dry. She had no more tears in her. She had been drained between my father and me.

"Aiden?" her lips trembled.

I couldn't tell her. I didn't want to cause her any more pain.

"Who's Matte? And why were you calling out for Billy? Aiden answer me, why were you calling out William's name?"

She stared at the stranger I had become. I didn't want to be a stranger. I wanted to be her son. I had to tell her.

"Mrs. Long, please step back," a doctor instructed my mother.

"Aiden, why do you want to kill yourself?" my mother begged. Her tone was getting increasingly agitated.

188

"Mrs. Long, please step out of the room. Shawn, please show Mrs. Long where she can wait."

A second doctor flashed my eyes with a bright light.

"Aiden!" I heard her scream from the hallway.

"Mommy… Mommy…" my brother followed them out the door.

I tried to lift my arms and legs, but the restraints made it impossible. My fingers tingled and sweat beaded at my forehead. My stomach was still turning, and I could feel puke traveling up my throat.

"Aiden, relax. Don't move, it will only make things more difficult. My name is Dr. Scott and this is my apprentice, Dr. Porter.

Dr. Scott was a short, round man with horseshoe pattern baldness while Dr. Porter was younger, slimmer and healthier looking. The young doctor wore tight grey slacks and a white plaid shirt with a bowtie. The older doctor had seen better days, his balding head and loose-fitting clothes didn't do him any favors.

"We need you to relax. Can you do that for us?" The round man cocked his head and beamed at me.

I took a deep breath and swallowed hard. Life had taught me that struggling always made things worse.

"Good man. Shawn, would you remove the restraints please," Dr. Scott ordered.

Both doctors stood at the edge of my bed, whispering and looking at charts in their hands. Shawn removed the restraints and allowed me to sit up. I wasn't ready for what followed.

"Aiden, we need to ask you some questions. Is that alright?" Dr. Scott asked.

I nodded, rubbing my wrists where the restraints had been.

"Were you attempting to take your life?" Dr. Scott asked.

I remained silent.

"Aiden, you had large amounts of fluoxetine as well as large amounts of LSD and traces of cocaine in your system when you were brought here. You were in a coma for three days. You nearly died," the young, stylish doctor said.

Silence followed. I wasn't sure what I should say. I was afraid to make things worse.

"Listen, we are not going to pester you at the moment, but it is our duty to inform you that following your medical care here you will be admitted to Providence DePaul Clinic for a mental health evaluation and rehabilitation." Dr. Porter adjusted his bowtie.

"You're sending me to a nuthouse? No, you can't. Not without my consent."

"Aiden, you tried killing yourself. You have no say in the matter," Dr. Scott said.

"You guys it was an accident... I needed to forget something, and I overdid it."

"We don't know that. And due to the drugs you used, we cannot trust you. That is why for your safety and the peace of mind of everyone in your life, we're sending you to get professional help. If everything goes well you'll be out in a couple of short weeks."

Dr. Scott ran a hand through his balding head and gripped the clipboard tightly with the other.

So many thoughts and emotions ran throughout my body and bottlenecked at my chest. I was suffocating and the room spun again. I was in deep shit.

This was all his fault!

"You can't do this. I won't let you!"

I screamed and jumped off the bed. Tubes came out of my arms, and instruments flew off the nightstand.

Shawn and a group of nurses rushed into my room and surrounded me. Hands gripped my body as Shawn injected a tranquilizer into my arm. My body began losing strength, one nerve ending at a time. Not even the years of drug abuse were enough to fight back the effects of the powerful sedative.

As the faces disappeared, I fell back into the dark hole Matte had created, the nightmare that harbored every memory of him good and bad.

Over the next few days, I was in and out of consciousness. I don't remember much. I have flashes of doctors and nurses in my room. They cleansed my skin with rags and warm water. They fed me through tubes and sedated me through IV. I was only awake for minutes at a time, at most.

I remember when the sedatives wore off enough to allow me limited control. I awoke to a bright room. The walls were white, and the blinds on the large windows sat open, allowing a view of the vibrant outside.

I wasn't restrained to the bed, and I had no tubes or needles in my arms. I sat up and removed the covers from my body. My legs were lazy, unresponsive to the commands sent from my brain. I was heavy from continuous sedation.

I attempted to move my legs again, still no response. I grabbed one and slid it off the bed, then grabbed the other to do the same thing. I was quickly stopped by a man dressed in white who came out of the restroom in the suite.

"Mr. Long, where do you think you're going?" he asked. His voice was deep and strong.

I looked back at him but couldn't reply. My tongue was numb. The man laid me back down, covering my legs with the blanket once again. He reached for nightstand phone and asked for Dr. Lucerne Heinz.

"Dr. Heinz will be with us in just a moment. Please be patient." He set the phone down and ran his hands over the bed, straightening my covers once again.

Part of me felt afraid of him. He was big and confident, the true definition of a man. He was different than any men I'd ever encountered. Although my body felt tired, I refused to close my eyes. I had to keep them on him. I had to be ready to fight him off at all costs.

"Mr. Long," a woman said walking into the room breaking the tense silence. She stopped at the foot of the bed and stared at me.

"May I call you Aiden?"

I nodded not looking away from the man in white.

"My name is Dr. Lucerne Heinz, I am a psychiatrist. I will be working with you to try to help you. How are you feeling today, Aiden?" she asked.

Her question went unanswered as I continued to stare at the man.

"Anthony, could you give us a moment please?" she asked.

The man nodded and left the room. My eyes followed him out the door.

"Aiden, do you feel more comfortable now?"

She stood directly in my field of view. I looked up and down at the woman. She didn't look like a doctor. She looked like someone's mom. Her hair was short and bobbed, speckled grey. She wore a black sweater and maroon pants. She held my file lightly in both of her hands, pressed against her chest.

"Why am I here? There is no need for it. You can't keep me without my consent."

"You are here because you tried taking your life, and I want to help you to feel like you don't have to."

She came to the other side of my bed.

"No one can help me. And I didn't try to kill myself. How many times do I have to tell you people that?"

"Well we're going to try. You have people who love you and care about you. That's why you are here, alive and on the way to recovery."

She put her left hand on the bed, testing to see how I'd react. The large rock on her wedding band reflected light onto the ceiling and walls. God, that would be a trip on some acid.

Her words sickened me. Something inside me repelled every one of them. No one ever loved or cared about me. Telling me that was a miserable lie, something she got paid to say.

"Come and take a seat with me. Let's have a chat. I would like to get to know you." She smiled. Her teeth were perfect and white.

Dr. Heinz reached her hand out to me. I took it, and she helped me out of bed.

"Can you walk, or do you need me to hold your hand?"

"I got it, thanks."

We walked side by side to the chairs by the window. My legs felt like noodles under my weight and I could feel puke traveling up my throat.

One thing I've noticed in life is time moves slower when you're walking into an event that will change you forever. It did when my uncle touched me the first time, when Kat sucked me off in her bathroom, when Vanessa gave me those white pills while we sat on the train tracks, when I noticed Matte staring at me across the library, when I woke up in Harry's office, and it did when I walked with Dr. Heinz to the chair.

192

I sat on the chair and looked at Dr. Heinz in the eyes for the first time. As I did, I knew everything would be different. I couldn't even prepare for what was to follow. I was a child again, naïve and ignorant.

"Aiden everything we do, we do for a reason. There is always something that moves us, motivates us, makes us do things. I believe you did what you did because you had enough. You keep saying it was an accident, and maybe it was. Maybe you were simply trying to forget, as you say. But I believe it was a cry for help."

She stopped to make sure I was following.

I tried to follow, but my eyes were distracted by the views out the window. The wind rattled the leaves on the trees. Squirrels scurried around carrying nuts and other little food-like objects they found on the ground. Birds built nests in the trees and fed their young. The grass was green, and the sky was blue without a single cloud in sight. Everything was alive. I was no longer in the dead city of West.

"Aiden?"

I glanced back at the doctor, meeting her eyes.

"I want you to tell me about Matte. Your mother believes he might be the reason you tried to take your life. She said you called out his name several times when she found you. There were missed calls and messages from him on your phone the day you were rushed to the hospital."

It was pointless to keep any information from her. I was vulnerable and in front of her; an open book. Aside from Harry, I had never spoken about Matte to anyone. He had always been my secret. Even the world he helped create was a secret. All of it was locked in my head with trails leading to my heart. I was a stranger to everyone since childhood. I was a stranger to Dr. Heinz.

How was I supposed to tell a stranger my secrets, my fears, my insecurities? Where was I supposed to start?

"Aiden, you can trust me. Everything you tell me is one more brick on the road to recovery," she said.

I sat quietly. How could I trust someone who was paid to listen to other people's problems? The profession seemed like a joke to me.

"Aiden, I've met countless people who thought similar things as I imagine you are now. You're thinking I don't care that this is just my job, right?"

She crossed her legs and rested the open file on her lap. Her words were calm and her breathing serene.

I remained silent. My eyes shot to the floor. I stared at the patterns the tiles created as the doctor continued to talk.

"This isn't just a job, Aiden, I do this because I truly care about people. I don't need the money; my husband is more than capable of providing for me and our children. I am here because I know some people are broken beyond repair. I am here because some people believe they don't have anyone in their lives that care about them. I am here because I want to be there for them when no one else will."

I looked at her now. I knew she was right. I wasn't completely alone, but I knew the few people in my life were incapable of helping me.

I had to try although I knew it wasn't going to be easy. But my life had never been easy. I opened my mouth and heard myself use the words that I swore no one would ever hear me speak.

"His name is Matte Black, like the paint. And I have been in love with him for the past year. I... I am a gay man, and I am in love with a man that will never be mine." My lips trembled. My life with Matte replayed in my mind as words continued to pour out of my mouth.

"It started out innocently. We hung out and listened to music. He was there to listen when I had something to say, and I loved him for it. We had sex. Then he revealed he had a girlfriend. And he would see us both, sometimes at the same time. He said he thought I would be better with them than out in the world doing drugs. I didn't know what we were, but we weren't what I wanted us to be."

I coughed and took a deep breath. My eyes watered but my lids kept them from spilling.

"He said he would break up with her, and he never did. He came and left, again and again. And I kept falling for him. I hate myself for falling for this guy. I hate the confusing feelings that have made my life a million times more difficult to live. I hate that I have always been his secret. I hate that his girlfriend has all the love that belongs to me. And I hate that this is the first time in years that I am completely sober, and I have to deal with all of this."

My eyelids gave in and tears ran down my face. I wiped my eyes on my bare arms. Dr. Heinz handed me a tissue, and I blew my nose on it.

"I met someone else. His name is Harry, he's a man of God. He's a good guy. We hung out a lot. We had sex a few times before he told me he loved me. I... I can't love him back. There's no room in my head or in my heart for him."

I paused to blow my nose again.

"Every time I thought I could replace Matte with him, I went running back to Matte. And Matte didn't even try to get us apart, which is the most infuriating thing. He didn't even have to try to get me back, he always had me. I hurt Harry... a lot. I know I'm a terrible person, I know that. I know that I am Harry's own Matte Black, and I hate myself for it. He deserves better. We both deserve better."

I was full-on sobbing now.

Every few minutes Dr. Heinz looked at me with the same look that I saw in the mirror. She felt my pain. She felt my struggles. She understood why I had to use drugs to help me get through the days. Not once did she ask me the cliché question: How does that make you feel?

And that made me feel like I mattered.

Dr. Heinz kept her composure. She sat straight with her back flat against the rest. Her face glowed with the light from outside. She closed the file on her lap and moved it to the table between us. She rubbed her hands together as if she had a soft clay ball between them.

"It's good that you understand what was wrong. It is good that you are open to the idea that, perhaps, Matte isn't good for you. I know understanding and coming to terms that some things are beyond our control is difficult, but that doesn't mean everything is lost. Yes, it sounds like maybe Matte used you, but he might feel otherwise. It sounds like he thought he was helping you. His heart might have been in the right place. As far as your relationship with Harry goes, it might not be completely over either. You know you did him wrong; have you tried apologizing?

Tell him how you feel about him and how you treated him. That might help him understand."

I wiped my eyes with a tissue and stared out the window. The tears kept coming. The more I wiped, the more came. It was pointless to even try to stop. Dr. Heinz wasn't taking sides. She didn't say Matte was bad, and she didn't say Harry was good. She even saw an out I had missed. I never reached out to Harry to try to make him understand that I never meant harm, we were just not meant to be. I looked back at her. She pressed her lips and pushed the box of tissues over to me.

Dr. Heinz waited a few minutes for me to control my emotions. When I finally stopped sobbing, she moved onto the next topic. It was the topic I hoped she would forget but was glad she didn't. I had been carrying the weight of years of abuse on my shoulders for far too long.

"We can talk more about them later. We've got nothing but time. Now, what can you tell me about William? He is your uncle, your mother's brother, correct?" She nodded once. "Your mother says he hasn't been around for years, so she finds it odd that you called out his name, and I agree. What can you tell me about him?"

My lips trembled, and my throat went dry. My uncle was how it all started. He was the reason I lived every day in a personal hell. He was the main reason I was broken and susceptible to further abuse from other people.

I told her about the baby watermelons, my grandmother taking care of me, and my father constantly beating the living shit out of my mother. But that was easy. What was really hard was telling her how my uncle raped me every chance he got for years. I told her how it felt to have his hands all over my body. I told her how he pushed his way inside me and the unbelievable pain and guilt he made me feel. I told her how I saw him everywhere I went, regardless of time and distance.

I told her how, just when I thought I had outgrown his desires, I fell into the hands of Kat, and how she continued what my uncle had started. I told her how I hated that my body always did what they wanted it to do. I hated my body for it. I told her how I kept going back to Kat, over and over, for years without knowing why.

"My life has been a disaster from birth. I know life isn't fair but it doesn't have to make me wish for death every day either. Sometimes I felt like I should've never been born. What is the point? Why did I have to open my eyes every morning just to see my dad beating my mom? Why did I have to go to school every day just to come home and get my uncle's dick in my mouth? Why did I have to go to Kat's every Friday night just so she could have her way with me?"

I stared down at the floor. My tears fell and soaked into my gown, disappearing completely. I coughed and blew my nose. I threw the tissue in the overflowing trash bin between the doctor and me.

I told Dr. Heinz about my first girlfriend. She was the one who introduced me to drugs. She was the first person who ever attempted to help me. The opioids she gave me relieved the years of abuse and the pain they brought. All I had to do to get them was fuck her. Every couple of years, a new girl showed up and with her, a new drug. Drugs and sex helped me forget the past, but they kept it in the present. It was a psychotic ride to hell, and I couldn't get off of it.

Dr. Heinz sat perfectly still. Her eyelids fought to hold back her tears. She had no more questions. She had found the root of the problem. She knew why I was a piece of broken glass cutting everyone around me. If there was any good in her, she would kill me and put me out of my misery.

Instead, she stood and leaned towards me. She hugged me with the tightest hug a human being could give. I knew she was breaking protocol, but she did it with the best intentions, not giving a crap what years of professional experience taught her.

"I am so sorry you encountered some of the worst monsters in this world. There are no words to explain how I feel for you. I will work my hardest to help you get better. I promise you that Aiden," she said through the tears.

This was the first day of my new life and it was a long one. We talked for hours. She went through every year of my life, again and again. She took countless notes and patiently waited every time I broke down.

That evening, Dr. Heinz helped me back to my bed. I signed the consent forms so she could notify my mother about everything before she left me to rest. I lay on my side facing the door and she covered me with the blanket. I saw her disappear into the bright light of the hallway like the angel she was.

She was the first person to show me sympathy since the days I thought Matte cared. I knew that my life was as about to change. Soon other counselors in the facility would know and come to offer support. My mother, my grandmother, and father would know. Would they wonder how I lived with such a secret life? Would they judge me? Perhaps hate me? Or even worse, want nothing to do with me?

I wondered what would happen to my uncle and Kat… would they go to prison? And I wondered what would happen to Matte. Would his life be destroyed since I confessed our short-lived affair? Would he hate me for falling in such deep love with him? Or would he pity me?

I had so many thoughts and questions in my head I thought it would explode. It pounded so hard my vision blurred every few seconds.

I couldn't even collect myself before my mother and Dr. Heinz came into the room. My mother didn't look much different. She had fixed her ponytail and perhaps had some coffee, but she still looked tired and drained.

Dr. Heinz walked out of the room, rubbing my mother's shoulder as they passed each other. My mother stood at the doorway, watching me with tears in her eyes and regret on her face. I knew the doctor had told her everything: my homosexual affair, my drug abuse, her brother's abuse, Kat's abuse. She didn't see the twenty-two-year-old me. Instead she saw the child that never got the chance to grow up. I was the little boy who lost his innocence to her blood relative.

She shook her head and sighed heavily before slowly stumbling towards me. She collapsed to the floor before my bed and exhaled.

"I'm… Aiden… I'm so sorry I let this happen," she cried. "I'm a horrible mother. I can't believe I let this happen to you."

I jumped out of bed, and fell to the floor with her, wishing I could take it back. I wanted her to be happy. Why did I always make her cry? I unleashed the worst possible pain on my own mother. In a way she had lost her son. I grew up dead. She didn't know me any more than I knew myself. I held her face and watched her die inside through her eyes. I wanted to make it all go away. I wanted to make it all better.

"It's not your fault... it's not your fault Mom... it's not..." I said.

She threw her arms around me and buried my head on her chest and continued to cry.

We held each other for a little while as the sun hid in the horizon. The years of separation dissolved, and she became my mother again. It would be a long road to recovery, but I knew we were taking the steps in the right direction.

The days that followed weren't easy by any means. I was expected to meet with Dr. Heinz once a day to talk about my thoughts. I had no idea what she wanted from me. What else could I say? The only thing in my head was Matte. I couldn't forget him just like that. So naturally, conversations with her always ended up with tears. Reliving my past without a future, in a strange place, surrounded by strange people, drained me.

Every day she tried to extinguish the fire in my heart, but the embers always reignited. Letting go was the hardest thing I ever attempted to do. She never gave up. She hacked at it every day. She was determined to save me. And after a while, she kinda did. I thought about everything less and less.

I thought about Matte less and less.

I started occupying my mind with mindless things such as drawing. I spent hours in the atrium looking out the windows, sketching squirrels and chipmunks in the yard. Their lives were so much simpler than mine. I put puzzles together and even helped the cleaning people clean up the dining area after we ate.

I had been in the recovery center for two weeks now. My mother visited three times. It was hard for her since she worked tirelessly to support the household. Without me there to help, she had taken on extra shifts serving at the truck stop restaurant.

But I appreciated the time she took to come by. She looked better every time I saw her. Although I knew she worked hard, she no longer had bags under her eyes. Her skin had returned to its normal complexion, and she wore clean, crisp clothes.

I cried less, so I naturally looked better. I could tell seeing me improve made her improve. When she came in and saw I wasn't an absolute mess, she smiled. She even brought my brother with her the third time she visited. He brought me a drawing he made for me after school that day.

"Aiden!" He came in running through the door.

He was taller and slimmer since the last time I spent any time with him.

"Hey, what's up man?"

"I'm not a man!" He looked at the floor shyly.

"Yes, you are, look at you. You're all grown up."

"No, I'm just a kid." He tried to hide his grin.

"So, what you got there?"

"It's you! I drew it for you."

I stared at the drawing. I was in cartoon form wearing a black suit, drawn in colored pencils. He had even attempted shading. Not bad.

"Do you like it?"

"Yes. I love it. Thank you."

I met a lot of people during my stay at Providence. Some of them were gone more than others. They left their hollow bodies scattered throughout the center. Some stared out the windows for hours. Others stared at the white walls while their lifeless heads floated on their bodies. I always wondered where they went. I wondered if they would ever find what they were looking for.

After a while I noticed some of them never came back. I knew they were lost in time, somewhere in their memories. I liked to imagine they were happy, together with whomever they needed to find.

Sometimes I wondered if I looked as dead as them when I left to find Matte in the depths of my mind. As hard as I tried not to let him, he popped into my head randomly.

Other patients were present more than me. They were normal, only at the rehab center to escape their daily lives. I met an interesting woman by the name of Larie. I called her "Larry" because that's how I thought her name was pronounced. But she liked me calling her Larry. She also liked talking to me. And I liked talking to her. She told me I reminded her of her lesbian lover, Lotiesse.

Larry was big, and her arms were covered in tattoos. She had short hair that she spiked up in all directions. And she was a little shorter than me. Larry was very social. She went around talking to everyone, gone or not.

We sat in the courtyard one day eating gelatin. Green was my favorite. It was a sunny beautiful day. Not too hot. Larry hated gelatin, so she gave me hers. I had finished mine and started on hers when she stopped talking. She leaned in and showed me her stowaway phone.

"How'd you get that in here?" I asked. My mouth was full of gelatin.

"I've got my ways. Check this out. This is my girlfriend Lotiesse. You remind me of her. She's weird like you. I think you two would be good friends.

I looked at the photo and instantly remembered Matte. It wasn't that Lotiesse looked like Matte. It was that Lotiesse loved Larry unconditionally, like I loved Matte.

"Why you getting all serious now?" She noticed my face changed as Matte entered my mind.

"Does this remind you of someone?"

"Yes." I looked away.

"A girl?"

I stared at the ground.

"A boy?"

I looked up. Bingo.

"Well, don't be shy now. Tell me about him."

I hesitated for a minute. But what did I have to lose? I had nearly died for the man, the least I do was tell people about him.

"His name is Matte Black, like the paint."

I held my trembling hands together trying to make them stop.

"I'm a man, and I am in love with a man. I met him at the library where I worked. He completely changed my life. He became my entire world. But, I wasn't his. One day he just up and left. I texted him and called him. I tried to hold on, I tried to make it work."

"Shit. Your first boyfriend?"

I nodded.

"Aiden, Aiden, Aiden… that was your mistake. You never fall in love with your first same sex partner. That's the number one rule about this. You're not over him, huh?"

I stared at the patio remembering him.

"No."

"I get it bro. I love Lotiesse. I love her smile, her goofiness, her style, but she just drives me crazy sometimes. She won't leave me alone. She texts me nonstop and calls me dozens of times a day."

"I'm sorry."

"Nah, bro, it's not your fault. Don't be sorry."

Larry explained to me how she had checked herself into the center several times over the past few years. She stayed for a couple weeks, then left. She treated the center like a vacation away from life. And in a way, it was. She needed time to heal herself before going back to her daily struggles. I liked Larry, not in an attractive way, but more in a person kind of way.

I knew I was changing. I mean, I never liked people, and now I was enjoying the company of strangers. It had to be progress.

Friday morning, after four weeks at Providence, I opened my eyes to the brightness of my room. It was the first time in a long, long time that I woke up without the instant feeling of worthlessness. It was also the first time I awoke to a thought that wasn't directly linked to Matte.

I lay in bed, thinking about my mother, and my brother. I thought about getting out and living a full day where everything was all about us as a family.

I thought about moving away from West and taking them with me. I thought about a future with them far away from my father, my uncle, and everything that ever hurt us as individuals and as a family. It was a future full of uncertainty and hope. It was the happiest moment I could ever imagine. But like every happy instance in my life, it was short-lived.

"Good morning…" I heard him say. I recognized his voice. I knew who he was before I even saw him.

"Jesus fucking Christ," I whispered.

My insides quickly ran hot. I felt my blood burning the same old, nearly erased path through my veins. Every memory I

202

had of him rushed back into my head. My eyes felt like they were melting and pouring out of my skull. My heart fell free from its place in my chest and into the pits of my stomach. I knew everything was about to change, again.

"Matte…"

Chapter 22

Where does the story end? Truth is, it doesn't. Traumatizing events such as abuse leave scars on your body. The wounds are often too deep to ever heal. It is difficult for those who haven't lived through the agonizing pain to understand it.

Those who abuse people, whether it's physical or mental, tear your spirits to shreds. They take from you what they want and don't need. They leave you trying to gather whatever pieces you can find to put yourself back together. You go on with life and try to make sense of it in your head. You go to extremes and make excuses to justify it. You convince yourself that it was your entire fault.

Then there's love. Because falling in love is inevitable. You give and give but never get back. Because you don't know any better. You don't know what you're worth, and you keep going and going only to keep them around. Love, is a big mistake. Because broken hearts never mend. They're patched by the love that others have to offer but they're never really repaired.

Some events follow you for the rest of your life. The story is written on your being. You tell it every time someone says the wrong thing or touches you the wrong way. You scream it every time you fall for the wrong person, because you do. You find yourself falling for anyone that gives you a hand and every time someone treats you like a real human being.

You're often blinded by what you think love is. You become so attached to someone who doesn't appreciate you that you miss out on what true love could be. Without knowing, you begin to hurt others, and so the cycle continues.

For a long time, I blamed my parents for bringing me into this world. I hated them for the shitty life they forced me to live. I blamed them every time we were hungry and had nothing to eat. I blamed them every time we had sleepless nights because of their pointless fights. But it wasn't their fault. They were merely trying to live and figure it out themselves. We, the offspring of the broken, are just a reflection of who they are.

All I ever wanted was to be normal. I wanted to be a normal kid with normal parents. I wanted to live a normal boring life. I wanted to walk, see, and feel the world as a heterosexual man without having to fight back the urges that came natural to me. But it just wasn't meant to be. My "normal" was different than everybody else's.

Matte walked into my room, scared and concerned. He stood in the doorway with his hands in his pockets, examining the entire room and stopping when his eyes met mine. They were red and wet. I knew he had been crying. His hair was shorter and slicked back into a pompadour. He wore a navy button-down shirt with black slacks. He looked so different, but he'd never looked more gorgeous in my eyes as he did that moment.

"Dude, what the hell?" he asked.

He closed the door behind him and strolled to my bed with his hands loosely at his sides. He sat, and I leaned up to meet him. We hugged tightly. He smelled so good, and his body felt even better in my arms. I didn't want to let him go, and from the way he held me, I knew he didn't either. We sat there holding each other for a few minutes before separating at the same time.

I stared at his face. There were many questions bouncing in his head, so many that he couldn't even formulate the sentences to spit them out. Instead he sat there staring back at me.

"Why?" he finally asked.

He didn't have to explain. I knew what the question meant. I couldn't lie to him. I couldn't deny that I had indeed tried taking my life.

"I… didn't mean for it to end like this. I wanted, needed to forget everything. My life is shit, you know that, man," I mumbled. "I didn't think I'd…"

I stopped before I finished the gruesome sentence.

"You didn't think you'd survive it?" he finished it for me.

I shook my head trying to control my emotions.

"Dude, what the fuck? Why did you want to kill yourself? I mean, I know things haven't always been good for you, but you didn't have to do this."

Matte knew about my shitty life conditions to some extent. I had briefly told him pieces and given him glimpses here and there. But, he didn't know about my uncle's abuse or that it extended through most of my childhood. He didn't know about Kat and that entire phase. He had no idea how strong my drug addiction really was. He also didn't know my father had put my mother in the hospital several times throughout my childhood and adulthood. And he most certainly didn't know how deeply I loved him.

Yes, he was aware that I loved him, that he was my first boyfriend, and that I valued our relationship deeply. But he didn't know how much I relied on him to aid my recovery. So, it surprised him that I wanted to take my life when everything fell on me all at once, and I wasn't strong enough to hold it back. Now that was out, I laid it all on the table for him to see.

"Matte, there's a lot about me that I never wanted you to know."

He stared into my eyes. His face was pained, and his breathing forced. He examined me carefully, trying to comprehend. My eyes shot to his hands resting on the bed. Tears welled up, and I opened my mouth.

"I was seven the first time it happened..." I said.

Without him asking, I told him about the years and years I had to live with my uncle raping me during the day, and my father beating my mother senseless during the night. I told him about the watermelons, my friends, the sleepovers, Kat, Kat's boyfriend, and how it all burned me out by the time I was sixteen. I told him about my first experience with drugs and how it started a new trend, junkie girlfriends that I used for drugs while they used me for sex.

I told him how refreshing it was when he came into my life, and how it changed my view on everything. I told him how I refused to be who he wanted me to be because of who I expected him to be. We were both wrong, we were both new chapters in each other's very different genre of books.

206

I paused several times to give him time to breathe and process things but not long enough for him to interject. I had to get it all out before I changed my mind and concealed the things he deserved to know. I saw my sadness reflected off his face as I recounted my horrific past.

After I told him everything, we continued to sit on the bed, inches from each other. He didn't know what to say, and I didn't know what to ask. I couldn't expect anything from him. It technically wasn't his fault I was there, even if I felt otherwise. But having to accept that is harder than it sounds. Having to accept that the person you love owes you nothing is one of the hardest things you'll ever endure.

"I'm really sorry," Matte said, reaching out to hold my hand. "I'm really sorry for everything you've ever had to deal with," he squeezed hard. "No one should ever feel like that, no one should ever have to live like that. I'm sorry that I wasn't there to help you with your uncle or help you with your shit at home."

He let go.

The second he released my hand, I felt him letting go of everything that once tied us together. He was sincerely empathetic for the life I lived, but he was also sorry because he was never who I needed him to be. The sterility of the room suddenly made me cold.

Matte stood and walked around the room for a few minutes. His footsteps echoed in my ears. He paused at the foot of the bed and stared into my eyes. His face was pale. His eyes sank to the floor, and he held onto the bed for support.

I wanted to know what was in his head. After all, I was happy he was there, but I wanted to know, what was next? I didn't know if I wanted to keep him in my life. I wasn't sure if I wanted to keep going through it all. I didn't know if *we* were strong enough for it.

I didn't want to guilt him into something that we would regret for the rest of our lives. But at the same time, I didn't know how to let him go. I didn't know if I could. I wasn't sure if I'd be able to live without him.

Matte closed his eyes and sighed. The clock ticked loudly in the silence of the room. When he reopened his eyes, tears escaped. He pressed his lips and swallowed hard.

"I'm sorry that I wasn't the person you hoped I could be." He held his hand to his chest. "I'm sorry for the mess I have caused. I shouldn't have let things get that far. I should've been smarter and kept it as a friendship." He shook his head. "I'm so sorry I can't be the man you want me to be dude, I really am." Tears rolled down his cheeks.

I didn't want to see him like that. If this was the end, I didn't want that to be my last image of him.

"I love you, but I can't be yours. I love Clarissa. She's pregnant... she's having a boy. We're starting a family. I'm going to be a father, man."

He sighed, rubbed his eyes and began to sob. It was the first and last time I ever saw him cry.

I wasn't sure what to feel. I was sideswiped by his words, distraught by his sincerity, and devastated by what was yet to come. I didn't want to see him like that. I didn't want him to feel bad for what he had done and what he was doing. It had to be done. Our lives were just beginning, and we couldn't keep letting our past interfere with our future. I didn't want to see him go, but I couldn't keep him from living the life he had already chosen to live. We had to end.

"I'm really happy for you," I said without realizing I, too, was crying.

He came to my side and hugged me.

"I'm really sorry Aiden. I love you."

I hugged him back, tighter. It was the last hug we would ever give each other.

"I love you Matte... I understand... we're just not meant to be," I said as clearly as I could.

After Matte left my hospital room, I never saw him again. It was a silent, mutual choice. Something inside allowed me to let him go even when I wasn't ready. But I do wonder about him from time to time. I wonder how his life turned out. I wonder if he and Clarissa got married, how their son is, and if they had any more children.

I wonder if life is as good to him as I hope it is.

I don't hate Matte for everything that happened between us. He wasn't the source of my depression. It just fed off his absence. I realized it was he who started the inevitable change that had to happen in my life. He kick-started my life the second he walked into it.

He showed me love, friendship, happiness, and betrayal. He gave me some of the best and worst days of my life. He pushed me to go to extremes, the only way I would ever learn.

But most importantly, he showed me there is more to life than waiting around to die.

It was all because of you, Matte Black.

ABOUT THE AUTHOR

Freddy Gutierrez is a Laboratory Supervisor who writes in his spare time. His writing explores complicated topics of life, such as sexual identity, abuse, love, and death. Freddy was born and raised in Texas. He has been living in Illinois since 2011 with his wife Holly and adorable dog Toki.